The
Consequences

by

Avis M. Adams

The Consequences

Cover Art by *Tina Lynn Stout*

The Wild Rose Press, Inc.
PO Box 708
Adams Basin, NY 14410-0708
Visit us at www.thewildrosepress.com

Publishing History
First Edition, 2024
Trade Paperback ISBN 978-1-5092-5820-8
Digital ISBN 978-1-5092-5821-5

Published in the United States of America

Dedication

This book is dedicated to my beta readers, Carl, Catherine, Melanie, and Ardi. Thanks for all of your support over the years, and your belief that I could write a novel worthy of going to print. Thanks to Ally Robertson, my editor, who has always supported me as I wade through this book-publishing-thing. Thanks to all the readers who loved The Incident. I hope you love The Consequences too. Thanks to all the people who read books and write reviews. You help writers more than you know. And finally, thanks Mom and Dad. You may not be here to read my books, but you helped shaped the woman I have become and the writer I've always wanted to be. I miss you both so much.

"Sooner or later we all sit down with our consequences." Robert Louis Stevenson.

"In times of war and hardship, hold your loved one's close because you never know when you might lose them." Unknown

Chapter One

Why did it have to be uphill all the way?

I stood on the bike pedal and pushed, letting my weight do the work, all the time Mr. G's words robbed me of breath, evaporated the air in my lungs: "It's colic again,

colic again,

colic again."

Horses survived colic all the time, but Shadow almost died last time, and this time, most of the roads were washed out or totally blocked with storm debris from El Primo.

Stupid storms—

No. No negative thoughts, not today. I turned up the corners of my mouth and forced a smile. It didn't help.

At least it was Saturday, a day at the barn, a run-my-fingers-through-her-mane day, a lope-on-the-trails day. But what if she—

Olivia, no negativity. Shadow had to be alive, and either way, I had to know the truth before I went back to school.

I'd missed so much already. How would I ever catch up in math? Recovery was too slow, and Emma said to rest another week, but Shadow couldn't wait.

I huffed and puffed in time to my pedaling, steering around potholes and branches. Some trees still stood beside the road, but gazing deeper into the forest showed tangles of trees and branches blown down by El Primo.

Life was nothing but hard since the storms. This hill wouldn't have been a problem in Grandpa Billy's truck, but it sat in the driveway dusty waiting for him to polish the green paint to a high sheen.

Grandpa.

Stupid hepatitis A virus stole my family.

I clamped my eyes shut. Maybe if the forest all around me stood tall and majestic, I could focus on the positive, but most of the trees had fallen in tangles of branches, and all I had to do was ride my bicycle around it all to get to Shadow.

But I couldn't fill my lungs with air, and these shallow breaths made me dizzy. Maybe I'd be in better shape if I could sleep through the night, but the nightmares…

Thank goodness Shadow didn't haunt my nightmares. Those spots were reserved for Grandpa Billy, Mom, and Dad.

Shadow was my hope, my carrot to survive. She'd kept me going through my illness, but could I save her?

Stupid colic.

Sweat ran from my temple, but I brushed my face on my shoulder and kept pedaling. She'd survived colic the last time, but barely. The vet said it could happen again, but—

Grandpa Billy's watch hung on my wrist like a weight. It slowed me down. The steep incline didn't help. I grunted, pressing with all my weight to keep my momentum.

I'd be there by now if I hadn't gotten sick. Mr. G's last radio message came the night I'd collapsed on the stairs, a week ago. Shadow could survive a week, right?

I clutched the handlebars and spurred myself to the top of the hill, my legs shaking with the effort.

Keep pedaling, legs. Just a little farther.

Highway 96 lay like an asphalt ribbon before me, filled with debris and deserted of anything automotive. I'd never get used to this post-storm stuff.

Birdsong floated on the fir-scented breeze with another sound I couldn't quite place. Was someone calling me? Please don't let it be someone calling me. I stopped, my breath raspy and loud, and checked Grandpa Billy's watch. 9:06 a.m.

A voice called, "O."

I glanced over my shoulder toward Cedarville. Was it the Dorkmeister?

"O."

Brian.

Argh. Mrs. Z did this. I despised being called "O," but he wouldn't stop. I clenched my teeth. Did he think giving me a nickname made us friends? It didn't.

Mrs. Z had nursed me to health, and I didn't have the strength to kick her out. Brian came with her. She took him in after his parents had died, about the time mine had, our guardian angel. Now I had to live in the same house with that dork.

Was I jealous of his energy? Ugh, yes. What made him think he even had a chance? I glared as he stood on his pedals and pumped with, as Grandpa Billy said, "more get-up-and-go" than I had.

Now I'd have to babysit his city-slicker ass. Geez.

I pushed my curly hair from my face. I couldn't even spend my birthday with my horse by myself. Who was I kidding? I was still weak. Mrs. Z didn't want me to make this trip, and this was my punishment.

A sign lay underneath the trees, partially covered with branches, pine needles, and leaves, but the morning sun still glowed off the letters.

CEDARVILLE

NEXT EXIT

I'd only gone a mile. Why was everything so difficult? Four more to the barn with the Dorkmeister in tow. Ugh.

I glared into the tangled forest. Classic Brian. Always trying to hang out with the juniors. Sophomore dork. I didn't want him anywhere near me.

Brian stopped his bike beside mine, huffing for air. "That's a workout." He gasped. "You're pretty strong for someone who's been sick for three weeks."

"What is Mrs. Z afraid of?"

"That you'll overdo it. That you'll be late for the party at Dr. Johnson's. Everyone's going to be there." He dismounted and pushed his kickstand down.

I clenched my teeth and rolled my eyes. "I'm not missing a cake with real sugar frosting."

He chuckled. "I didn't think so."

Why didn't he just go home? Grandpa Billy had always stuck up for Brian, said Brian would be a leader someday. I doubted that, but I couldn't argue with Grandpa. He didn't trust Perry. He'd quote something from Robert Louis Stevenson about sitting down with our consequences.

Consequences. He'd been right about Perry and the storms. I couldn't let my guard down, because caring about people was too difficult, and I wouldn't survive losing another person.

"I told her I'd bring you back before noon." He wore

that dorky smile like a badge of honor.

"You'll do what?" I clenched my fists. What nerve. "There is no 'we.' " I glared at him. "Why do you follow me around all the time?"

Grandpa's spirit was following me around today. He'd have said, "Don't react, respond. A reaction can hurt, but a response can heal." Right, Grandpa.

I blinked and counted to five, repeating. Respond. Don't react. Respond. It was too late, though. I'd reacted.

A crow swooped over my head with a loud ca-caw. It flapped its wings and disappeared into the branches of a tall fir, and I cringed. Was it the same crow that had called to me in my nightmares? The crow that had called three times outside Grandpa Billy's window when he'd passed. I didn't know if it was the same crow, but it had called three times when Dad passed and then Mom, as if it were calling their souls to leave me.

It was just a crow. No one was going to die. I opened my mouth to speak.

Brian blurted, "Did you see that crow? Just like when your—"

I scowled at him. "Don't say it." He was there when Grandpa Billy had died, so was the crow. Since when had I become superstitious?

I clamped my mouth shut and shuddered. My eye lids hung, heavy with grief, and my head pounded with my pulse. Why had it called three times at each death? I swayed.

"Hey." Brian held out a hand and grabbed my arm. "You're not well enough to ride to the barn, you know."

I pulled my arm away. "What do you know? A little flu isn't stopping me." I forced the words out, not ready to admit he might be right. "Shadow has colic."

"You had novel hepatitis A, not the flu."

"Ugh." I turned to stomp away, but he kept talking.

"And look at this log pile?" He frowned.

I glanced past the pile of debris and logs that blocked the road. Beyond it, 96 lay in stretches of cleared asphalt between logs that blocked the road. Was it like this all the way to Silver Springs Farm and Shadow? Why did he have to be such a downer?

"My dad oversaw the crews clearing the trees, remember?" I put my hands to my face.

Brian shuffled his feet.

I sighed. Why did he have to care about me? I couldn't afford to care about him or anyone, not after all the death, not after—

Perry Brewster. My chest constricted. The best-looking guy in the senior class, and he'd chosen me. Mom was furious, and Grandpa didn't approve, but Perry was a force I didn't even try to resist.

The last thing I needed right now was another boyfriend. My breath caught in my throat. I was still raw after Perry. I lifted my bike and pushed it around a fallen tree. Why had Perry changed after his mom passed? Grandpa Billy and I had sat two rows behind him at her funeral. It was the last time he spoke to me, but I could tell something was wrong. I waited for him to get over his grief and come back to me, but I was hit by my own grief storm and quit caring.

I walked around in a fever, alone in our big house. Grief canceled Perry's rejection. Then Dr. Johnson diagnosed, "Novel hepatitis A virus," and I collapsed.

Novel HAV. What was "novel" about a disease? Emma said "novel" meant we had no immunity. All I knew was I had zero immunity to grief, and Shadow was all that kept me going.

I might shatter into a million tiny pieces if she's gone too.

"I need to get to the barn." I glared at Brian. "She'll fight to live if I'm there." I lifted my bike from the ground and mounted, then stood on my pedals, pressing with all my weight.

The crow glided between the trees left standing, and a tremor ran through me. I pedaled harder past trees laying on the ground in a tangle and cordwood stacked by Dad's road-clearing crew. Why didn't they come back? Because of them, I had to pull my bike over all these logs.

"Hold up." Brian pulled his bike in front of me.

"Now what?" I scowled at him.

"I just need to rest a minute." He pulled out a water bottle and took a swig.

He meant he needed me to rest, but Dr. Johnson said to do what I was able to do, even if I was exhausted. My own doctor would know better than some dork on a bike.

"Fine." I swung my pack from my shoulder. Two could play at this game. I reached into my pack for my water bottle. My fingers brushed a book cover, my journal. Dr. Johnson said writing might be cathartic and help me with my "grief." Perry had surprised me with it on my birthday last April. I ran my hand over the cover. That had been a year ago.

I pulled out my water and took a deep swig. The Cascade foothills rolled from dark to lighter blue as they rose higher into the mountains, and I drank in the sweet mountain air. Brian kept his distance when we rode past the forest ranger station. Maybe he was smarter than I gave him credit for?

I slowed down by the sign I'd taken for granted until now.

Mount Rainier National Park

Mother Nature's Playground

Our playground. I glanced behind me. Brian was staring at the abandoned station. Dad had kept this place running, but the windows remained dark since his—

I pressed on. Shadow had to be alive.

The cloud cover grew thicker, and the temperature dropped, but sweat trickled down my back all the same. I wiped my nose on the back of my sleeve. My ribs ached on my upper right side. Mrs. Z said grief had lowered my immune system. I was so sick of her harping on about the seven stages of grief.

I was stuck on four. Depression, reflection, loneliness. Ugh. It was like that E. E. Cummings poem, "Loneliness." It seemed more like an anagram, a word game, than a poem. Mr. Woods loved that poem. I sighed. Sometimes, memories of life before El Primo helped, but not now.

****

I pedaled faster, gliding around a bend in the road.

"O." Brian pointed at something under a tangle of branches. A sign that read Silver Springs Stable.

Shadow.

I raced past Brian and turned down the next dirt lane to the barn. My heart raced and my legs ached. I'd made it.

Mr. Grady stood, his baseball cap on backward, per usual. I waved, but he didn't wave back. His overalls bagged around his knees, and his coat slouched off his bony shoulders. He looked grayer, older than the last time I'd seen him. Shading his eyes with his hand, he scowled. Didn't he recognize me?

"Mr. G, it's Olivia." I scanned the paddocks. No Shadow. Why wasn't she outside?

Hands on hips, he took a step toward me, a smile growing on his face, then disappearing. He pulled his cap off his head.

"Well, I'll be darned. Miss Olivia. I didn't recognize you." Mr. G frowned. "You've been sick. You're so thin."

"You too." I wanted to hug him, but first I needed to find Shadow. "Where is she? Did the vet get here in time?" I scanned the upper pastures, no gray mare. A sorrel and three bays stood heads hanging, ribs showing. My vision clouded. "Shadow."

No. The world spun as my arms hung like weights, Grandpa Billy's wristwatch heavy on my wrist.

Mr. G stared at his boots. He'd lost people too, but I couldn't stop searching for my last link to "normal." Shadow could not be dead.

"I heard about Grandpa Billy. I'm sorry—" He ran his fingers through his gray hair. "I thought that old man would live forever. He should have." The dark bags under his eyes spoke of losses too heavy to carry.

A jolt ran through me, and I sobbed. "Shadow." I dropped my bike and raced to the barn. She'd be in her stall, right?

The brakes on Brian's bike squealed as he stopped in front of Mr. G. "Hey. I'm Brian. She calls you Mr. G, but I can't call her 'O'? What's she—"

"Give her a moment, son."

What a dork.

I slipped through the small space between the big sliding doors of the barn and walked as if in a trance into

9

the barn and down the aisle to Shadow's stall. Her name tag hung on the door. Dust covered the shavings, and cobwebs filled the corners. Mr. G's message had come before I got sick, and now I was too late. I dropped to the dusty shavings and covered my face with my hands.

Chapter Two

Birds warbled in the trees outside Emma's bedroom. The sun should cheer her, but with all the deaths, no one was in a party mood.

She rolled her shoulders, repeating Dr. Johnson's mantra. "You can't resurrect the dead, but you can try to save the living." The sanctity of life meant something to her, but when would they clear the roads, and how did they save lives without the supplies they needed?

It had been seventeen months since the last monster storm, and she'd grown accustomed to life without electricity or cell phones or flush toilets, but what she really missed was streaming her shows. She could have lost herself in a good horror film instead of the horror of this new normal, but it was futile to harp on what they'd lost.

She sighed. "I'm off."

"Don't work too hard." Mom's voice came from the backyard. She was working in the greenhouse again.

Emma let the door click behind her and reached for her bicycle. The April weather promised warm days, and a bike ride would get her to the Cedarville Health Clinic early, giving her extra time to check her tests from yesterday.

She scanned the street for Josh, but he wasn't coming today to walk with her to the clinic. Maybe she'd walk her bike back with him this evening. Better yet, if it wasn't raining, they could walk through the park and stop by the place he'd proposed.

She sighed. Josh would greet neighbors, and she'd steer around sheep and cattle droppings. Livestock roamed free range through parks and yards now, and butchering day was a town feast day. Virg would have enough animal hides to make shoes and clothes soon.

Damn those monster storms. None of this would have happened if—

El Primo. The perfect scapegoat for everything bad in her life. It had caused all this chaos, right?

Dr. Woolf and Josh had kept Grandpa Woolf's radio on. They shared transmissions at the town halls. The storms had affected the West Coast inland, but the East Coast had been wiped out too. She'd sat numb in her seat as Dr. Woolf read his transmissions. No more Wall Street, no more grocery store chains, no more European vacations.

Did FEMA even exist anymore?

She gazed at the cleared streets and tidy yards. Some roofs were patched, some had new wood framed windows, but rebuilding had new rules. Supplies couldn't get through the mudslides, so wood and nails were in short supply. And with no electricity for power tools, everything took longer or didn't get done at all.

She could tolerate broken down fences and roads blocked with debris. Those things could be fixed eventually, but when the medicine ran out, and people started dying, she'd had enough. She'd marched to the clinic and volunteered. If she joined the doctor, maybe she could help save people.

Emma coasted her bicycle around a corner and

braked in front of the Cedarville Clinic. The hospital stood across the street, untouched by the storms, a minor miracle. Had it been three months already since she'd joined Dr. Johnson? He took her on rounds, teaching her as they went. She sighed.

Medicine was her calling now, and she loved the labs, with their microscopes and Petri dishes. When would the new doctor arrive? She was running low on reagent, but they had plenty in Franklin, and Dr. Nordby was supposed to bring more. The testing could continue only because Dr. Johnson rationed gas to run the equipment used to identify waterborne illnesses, E. coli and novel hepatitis A virus.

Novel HAV. A tremor ran through her. They'd run out of medicines to treat these viruses, and the result was death. Water sanitation was all they talked about at the town halls. Dr. Johnson reported deaths due to E. coli and dysentery. Then he found novel HAV in a test. This was third world stuff, right? He relied more and more on herbs like milk thistle for treating patients, but the clinic and hospital were running out of that too.

Rumor had it that the new doctor was bringing milk thistle with her, too, but shouldn't she be here by now? Maybe it was all the washouts on 96. Dr. Nordby might be trapped on the east side of Chinook Pass.

Emma read Dr. Johnson's instructions: mix the herb in a pot of tea, or sprinkle the powder on food. If in tincture form, put drops in clean water. She couldn't scan the weight chart for doses. The trick was which medicinal herbs to harvest and dry before winter and the end of the growing season, which was yet another learning curve.

Waterborne illnesses were invisible and deadly if

not treated correctly. E. coli outbreaks compounded the novel HAV outbreak. Emma sighed. Her mom had recovered, but almost one-third of Cedarville…so many funerals.

Cedarville seemed to be shrinking as people left to join family members elsewhere. Migrations they were called, groups of folks on the move, but they brought news of washouts on I-5 from Portland, flooding from the Skagit and Snoqualmie Rivers, then road slides from Chinook to Lookout Pass, flooding in Chicago, and the list went on. How did they get anywhere with all that destruction?

She didn't blame people for leaving, but there was safety in numbers. That's what got her through El Primo with Lilli and Jade, and at this point, running didn't solve anything. It only left communities like Cedarville with less of their most important resource, people.

Her heart raced, and she inhaled an unsteady breath. She gazed at the mountains and concentrated on Dr. Johnson's relaxation technique. It helped stop her from focusing on disasters and death.

PTSD. Life overwhelmed her sometimes, but hope came with the new doctor, right?

She closed her eyes. What was it Dr. Woolf had said about consequences? That the consequences we suffered now were brought on by the storms, and they were the consequence of decisions made by big corporations influencing elected officials, who either didn't know what they were doing or didn't care.

Smart man that Dr. Woolf.

Emma needed someone to blame, but the blame always came back to El Primo.

She adjusted her hand on the handlebars, and her

ring caught on the wrap. She'd have to retape her bike handle, but the sparkly distraction of the diamond glittering in the sunshine made everything okay, and so did Josh.

Chapter Three

I pulled the stall door open and circled the stall as though I might find her in a corner. I left the stall, my tears spent, and meandered the center aisle of the barn in a daze. Old Charlie hung his palomino head over a stall door. I cracked the heavy door at the end of the aisle to check the back pasture, but no Shadow.

I'd dreamed of this day. Of finding Shadow recovered and waiting for me. It had kept me fighting for health when I was sick, but in the back of my mind, I'd dreaded that I was already too late. My head swam with the jagged realization. I clenched my teeth and gazed at the roof beams filled with birds' nests and spiderwebs.

"Shadow—"

My voice echoed off the wall. A response came from one of the stalls down the aisle. Who was left? Of course. Old Charlie poked his head over the stall door. I ran my fingers over his velvet-soft muzzle. A rustling drew me to the next stall where a thin paint horse pushed his glossy black head toward me, his ears pricked forward.

"Top Hat?"

He snorted.

"What happened to you?" He blew hair into my face. I caressed his glossy black face. He licked the salt from my palm. "How come the ornery ones always survive?" He blinked. I opened the stall door, and he let me wrap my arms around his white neck. I pushed my nose under his mane, ignoring the sting behind my eyes.

Top Hat. My first lesson horse, my first fall onto the hard ground, my first rolling canter down the trails. He wasn't Shadow, but he was warm and alive and familiar. I melted into him, and the aroma of horse dander and fresh air filled my senses. He nuzzled my shoulder.

I squeezed my eyes shut and closed my heart to the pain. Tears wouldn't bring Shadow back. I counted backward from one hundred, like Grandpa taught me to do when the world threatened to swallow me whole. Mr. G and Brian reached me at number thirty-six.

"I would have sent word, but my radio went out after that last message."

I nodded, my arms still around Top Hat's neck. "I guess I already knew she was gone."

"I'm ever so sorry." He twisted his hat in his hands.

"Me too." A pain constricted my chest as I pressed my nose into Top Hat's neck. I patted him, then joined Mr. G in the aisle, closing the stall door behind me. Top Hat pushed his nose into Mr. G's shoulder.

I wiped my eyes and tried to smile. "So, where's Mrs. G and Ms. Debbie?"

Mr. G stood, wringing his hat in his hands. "Ms. Debbie stayed and helped with Mabel, but—" He scrutinized his boots.

Brian ambled toward us. "Who's Ms. Debbie and—"

"Brian." I scowled at him, shaking my head until he backed away and wandered out of the barn. *Dork. Always a pain in my ass.*

I placed a hand on Mr. G's arm. "I can't believe it.

I'm so sorry, Mr. G."

His eyes turned glossy, but no tears fell. He cleared his throat, and I waited for him to make eye contact. He didn't.

"I sent Hank and Jeff home. Ms. Debbie stayed until…"

He wiped his eyes. "She left after that." He scanned the barn, his calloused hands hanging at his side. "I can't run this place alone. It's too much."

I followed his gaze to the wheelbarrow full of manure, and the small stack of hay in the feed room. Mr. G led me outside. I stood by the barn door as Mount Rainier loomed in the distance under a blue sky filled with fluffy clouds, a perfect April day. The breeze held the sweet scent of cottonwood buds forming on the trees.

I sighed and pulled my gaze from the mountain. This day was turning into a reenactment of one of my nightmares. Perfect? It was anything but.

"I can help—" I glanced at Brian. "—and so can he. What do you need?"

Mr. G shook out his cap and stuffed it on his head. "Well…"

My stomach tightened as he struggled for the words to ask me for help.

Brian approached me and Mr. G. Mr. G glanced at Brian and cleared his throat. I tensed. If he needed something, why didn't he just ask?

"Old Charlie was the fattest of them all, remember? I've released so many horses. Kept the ones I couldn't bear to part with, but I'll have to turn them all out to fend for themselves soon. They're starving, and I don't want to—"

I froze. *Kill them?*

"No." I frowned, glancing into the barn.

Mr. G shifted from one foot to the other. "I need more hay or…" His voice cracked.

"How do we get more?" Brian patted Top Hat on the neck.

"It's not that simple. Mr. Coffey might have extra, but with my radio out, I can't contact him." He twisted his cap.

I put a hand to my pounding head.

Mr. G held up his hands. "I'd go myself, but Angel is due to foal any time now, and she always needs help. She was Mabel's." He paused and cleared his throat. "I can't lose her."

Just saying Mabel's name was difficult for him. I'd kept Shadow alive in my mind, and it had kept me going, and now Mr. G needed Angel. We had to save her and that foal.

"If you could take a message to Mr. Coffey?" He scrunched his hat into a ball.

I peered at Mr. G, his gray hair and large nose were just like Grandpa's. I rubbed my arms to get the blood flowing. I swallowed as a chill shook me. I was just tired, right?

"We can go." Brian stepped forward. "It's just down the road, isn't it?"

"We can what?" What made him think he could speak for me? What the—

Mr. G reached out a hand and clasped Brian's, and they shook. I raised a hand to object, but I couldn't speak.

"Bless you." Mr. G patted Brian's shoulder.

"We can be there and back before you know it." Brian glanced at me, then to Mr. G.

"But—" The words stuck in my throat as my knees

buckled.

****

I cracked my eyes open. The sun shone through the window, casting shadows across the wood dining room floor. Mr. G knelt beside me. I ran my hand over the blanket. How did I end up inside on the couch? Did I faint?

"Here. Sip this." Mr. G held up a cup of water to my lips.

Cool water ran down my chin, and I sat, taking the glass from Mr. G. I gulped it down. Brian frowned at me like a déjà vu moment of Mrs. Z when I was sick. I hated that look.

I'd show him. I wasn't sick anymore, right? I tried to sit, but the world tilted. I sank back, and the rotating room stopped spinning.

"Slow down, Miss Olivia." Mr. G placed a hand on my shoulder.

I wanted to smile to reassure him, but I'm pretty sure I grimaced instead. Who was I kidding? I was not fine, but I nodded as if moving through cement. Pushing myself to sit, I hugged my knees to my chest, hiding my hot face. I'd never fainted in my life, and it left me dizzy, weak. "How long was I out?"

Mr. G took the glass, refilled it, and placed it on the coffee table. "Not long. A couple minutes maybe. Your friend blames himself. Said he won't leave without you."

Brian shifted from foot to foot.

I shook my head. "What? But your horses need that hay."

"You need rest, and the horses will be fine for another day. Brian's helping me mend the fence on that east pasture. I can let the horses out, and that will buy me some time until Mr. Coffey brings the hay."

"Rest." I melted into the couch, folding my arms over my stomach. "Sounds good right about now."

Mr. G stood. "I'll check on you in a bit." He strolled out the front door.

Brian refused to leave without me? I would have left him in a hot minute. Or would I? I stared out the window at the billowing clouds riding the thermals high above.

I drank from the glass Mr. G had left beside me. The water soaked into my cells, giving me strength.

The picture window in Mr. G's living room framed Mount Rainier. She stood like a snow queen under a sky so blue it hurt my eyes. My head ached but no longer pounded, and I pressed the heel of my hand against a temple.

I couldn't just lay here. I rose from the couch and wandered outside to the fence where Angel stood. A nicker rumbled in her chest as she sniffed my hand. "Sorry. No carrots."

I had to save her. She was the mother hen of the barn, the only one Shadow would allow to share her paddock.

Shadow.

I was not prepared for any of this. I clamped my eyes shut. How could anything ever live in my empty chest again? I checked my watch, 10:12 a.m. I gazed at the blue sky with the fluffy clouds, and let them blur as Mr. G's words played in my mind. *The horses will starve.* All I had to do was get a message to Cedar Hills Farm and get home in time for the party.

Easy peasy, but it was uphill all the way.

Chapter Four

Mr. G fed us scrambled eggs and toast, and Brian helped him clean up. I sat on the couch, frowning. Brian had become Mr. G's right-hand man, and I had become the weak link.

"Ready, Miss Olivia?" Mr. G hung the dish towel on a hook.

I nodded, and I grabbed my backpack. I followed them out of the house and across the yard. The lunch had given me energy, but I hated to eat Mr. G's food. He was so thin.

He put a hand on Brian's shoulder. I frowned. *Guys.*

"You can't miss the big red barn. Cedar Hills Farm is painted on the roof, and his name is Samson Coffey." Mr. G wadded his hat in his hands.

Brian's eyes twinkled as he smiled. "Samson? Like Delilah's Samson?"

Mr. G chuckled. "Yep. Samson is bald." His eyes gleamed with relief.

"Good one." Brian nodded.

Leave it to Brian to crack a joke. I tried to smile, but lightheadedness made my vision swim. Was I ready for this? No, but I wanted to help save the horses, for Shadow's sake. We'd deliver Mr. G's message to Samson, then get back home in time for my birthday party this afternoon. I gazed into the distant mountains.

Mrs. Z was going to kill us if we were late, but—

Gravel crunched under my shoes. Brian stopped, and I bumped into him.

"What's up?" I peered over his shoulder.

He pointed. I followed his finger and gasped. "Our bikes." We'd leaned them against the barn, but they were gone.

"Dag-nab it." Mr. G slapped his hat on his thigh. "Those thieving coyotes. I knew I should have locked those bikes in the barn."

"Thieving coyotes?" Brian said.

"Aaron and Perry Brewster. They steal anything that isn't nailed down. They must have snuck in here while we were in the house and stole them."

"The Brewsters? How do you know it was them?" My heart pounded like a fist against my ribs. Did Mr. G know about me and Perry? "Perry wouldn't do this, but his little brother, Aaron, is crazy." I put a hand to my head. Would Perry steal our bikes? Maybe he would for Aaron.

"I started missing things about two months ago, so I slept in the barn and caught those two red-handed. They got away with my garden wagon. I need that thing."

"How will we get to Mr. Coffey's without bikes?" Cedar Hills Farm was about one and a half miles, then the four and a half miles home. I wouldn't make it.

Mr. G slapped his hat against his leg. "I have an idea. You two can ride."

"Ride?" Brian's blank gaze made me scoff.

"Horses. The trail from the upper pasture is a shortcut. You can go as the crow flies and cut off a half mile."

Brian smiled from ear to ear, and I scowled,

imagining Brian on a horse.

"Have you ever ridden?"

He shoved his hands deep in his pockets, holding his lips in a flat line. He had no idea what lay in store, saddle sores being the least of his surprises.

Mr. G walked to the barn, slid the giant door back. It glided with a whoosh. The horses whinnied, and heads reached over stall doors.

Mr. G went into farm-manager mode. "Chip's only green broke. He'll buck you off before you get to the trailhead. Magic is too spirited, even for Miss Olivia." Mr. G scratched his head.

Old Charlie popped his head over the stall door. "The babysitter," we called him, but I'd never tell Brian that.

Mr. G patted the palomino's neck. "Old Charlie for Brian, and Top Hat for Miss Olivia."

Top Hat poked his head out and nickered. I'd get to ride the trails after all, but I'd be a babysitter like Old Charlie. We'd need more than horses, though, if Aaron Brewster was still out there. Aaron had never liked me, but he didn't like anyone. Perry had once cared for me, so maybe that counted for something. Besides, he wouldn't hurt me, would he? I pressed my hand against a pain in my chest and stared into the trees that covered the hill above Silver Springs Stable.

****

I adjusted my helmet and slipped my backpack on with the pack in the front. Ms. Debbie had taught us that so I could grab water or a snack without dismounting. I put my left foot in the stirrup and swung my right leg over Top Hat's back. He tossed his head. The wooziness had disappeared, and I collected Top Hat and steered him toward the gate. Top Hat danced sideways, and I tightened the reins to hold him back. I swayed with each prancing step and beamed.

I'd missed this, sitting high off the ground, the roll of the horse's body as it moved. I couldn't wait to canter. I inhaled the sweet mountain air. Brian stumbled, and Mr. G rushed to his side.

"Let me give you a leg up, Brian." Mr. G showed Brian how to hold the reins and how to squeeze his legs to get Old Charlie to walk.

I would give my first riding lesson today. Brian had better hold on tight.

"Be safe, and happy trails." Mr. G patted Old Charlie's rump as he ambled through the gate. "Maybe there'll be a foal when you get back."

I saluted Mr. G as I nudged Top Hat, whose ears pricked up as he walked through the gate Mr. G held.

"Bye." Brian spoke through clenched teeth and clung to the saddle. He hunched over Old Charlie's neck. Old Charlie plodded behind Top Hat, and my blood raced through my veins.

****

The brisk morning air hit my neck, and I shivered, zipping my jacket to my chin. I held up my wrist to check the time, 11:48 a.m. We were making good time. It wasn't even noon, and with any luck, we'd be home in time for a late lunch. I glanced back, and Brian's helmet flopped down over his eyes.

I sighed. The lesson began now. I stopped by the fence and dismounted, throwing the reins over the fence. "Good boy," I murmured, patting Top Hat's shoulder. "Can you see anything through your helmet?"

"Not a thing." Brian chuckled, braying like a

donkey. Old Charlie stopped, and Brian uncrunched his shoulders.

"We need to tighten your chin strap so you can see. You don't want to rub all the hair off your head, do you?"

He shook his head, the helmet wobbling. He slipped it over his head without unlatching the chin strap.

I tightened the strap and handed it to him. "Try that. Your chin should be snug in that plastic cup."

He clicked the strap and shook his head. The helmet fit snug. "Wow. I can see." He scanned the open view and pointed into the distance. "Man, look at Mount Rainier."

I turned. Mr. G's fenced pastures and barn lay sprawled before me, and beyond that stood Mount Rainier, the majestic queen. At least some things hadn't changed. I mounted and patted Top Hat's neck, then nudged him into a walk.

We rode in silence through the scraggly trees and over logs to the gate at the top of the pasture, the only sound birdsong and the creak of saddle leather. The glaciers sparkled like royal jewels.

We rode to the fence, and I sidestepped Top Hat to a metal gate. I reached down and unlatched it, grabbed the top rail, and walked the horse through, holding it open for Old Charlie and Brian.

"Nice. How'd you do that? You didn't even get off?" Brian's mouth hung open, but no words came out as I nudged Top Hat to sidestep so I could latch the gate.

"What?" I stared at him. I'd never get used to his questions, his reach for a connection between us. He stared back like a dork. I looked away first this time.

"It's like he could read your mind. You didn't say anything, and he turned and walked sideways and opened the gate—" He shook his head. "—like magic."

"What is it with you and magic?" I shook my head but couldn't stop the smile forming on my lips. Everything about horses was magical to me, so I was one to talk.

"Will you teach me? I want to know the right way to ride." He leaned forward in the saddle.

My face grew warm, and I cleared my throat. He was making every mistake a new rider could make. "To begin with, you don't want to let your reins hang so loose."

As if on cue, Old Charlie dropped his head and started pulling grass into his mouth as fast as he could. Then he stepped on a rein, and his head flew up in surprise. Brian wobbled in the saddle and dropped one. He slipped in the saddle trying to catch it.

"Whoa." He clung to the saddle horn.

"Grab that loose rein before he breaks it, and shorten them in your hands so they are tighter. That way he'll raise his head." I waited for him to fall off as Old Charlie pushed against the bit with his nose. The old horse didn't want to lift his head, but Brian pulled the reins tight.

"Don't jerk on his mouth."

Brian released his hold a little.

"He's not hungry. He's testing you." I resisted grabbing the reins from him and just leading him down the trail.

"How's that?" Brian turned to me and chuckled.

Old Charlie stood, ears flat back, and stomped his back hoof on the ground in frustration.

"You've got an F so far."

"F? Was this a test?" Brian loosened his reins, and Old Charlie pushed his nose out, shaking his head.

"You have to pay attention to his body language.

27

See his ears? He's angry."

"Is he mad at me?" Brian tightened the reins with both fists at eye level, his eyes as big as saucers. "Is he going to buck me off?"

This was going to be more fun than I thought. I kept my expression blank. "No, but you need to show him who's boss, Brian." I stood in my stirrups, and Top Hat took a step forward. I checked him, and he stood still. It came to me like second nature, and the only way Brian would learn was by doing.

"Look, if you let him stop and eat whenever he wants, he'll try to get away with something else later. Just sit upright and keep your reins short, like mine, so he can't reach down and eat while you're riding."

Brian pulled the reins taut and sat straight in the saddle.

"That's better." I nodded. "Old Charlie has learned some bad tricks over the years, and he can tell you're a newbie."

"A what?"

"That you've never ridden before, but we'll show him." I smiled. How was that for teaching? If we made it to Cedar Farm, it would be a miracle.

"What else does he know?"

"He knows when you're afraid, but he'll take care of you if you treat him with respect. He's a big softie."

"Hmm." Brian tilted his head.

I nudged Top Hat back onto the trail. We rode into a tangled forest. The storms had uprooted trees, and they laid in piles on the hillside. The road crews had cleared most of the roads and trails, so Brian might not have to learn to jump. Wait. Did that mean I cared about him falling off?

Nah.

Chapter Five

Birdcalls filtered over the valley, and a crow sent a warning call from a branch high above us. Chipmunks chattered as we passed. I watched for signs of cougar or coyotes. The last thing I needed was for one of the horses to spook. Would Brian survive this ride?

He needed lessons while things were calm. I turned in the saddle. "Let's trot."

"Trot?"

"Yea, a slow run, like a jog."

He ran a finger under the chin strap of his helmet. "Okay?"

"A trot is jerky, so we'll work on your balance." I squeezed Top Hat with my calves, and he trotted down the trail, ears perked forward. I turned in the saddle.

Brian hunched over Old Charlie's neck. He clung to the saddle horn and bounced a foot off the seat with each of Charlie's steps.

"No, no, no." I stopped Top Hat.

Brian bounced out of the saddle and landed in a heap on the trail.

I grimaced. "We could—"

"No, I got this." He put his foot in the stirrup and pulled himself back into the saddle as Old Charlie ate grass. "Let's go again." He kicked Old Charlie's sides.

"It's your funeral," I muttered under my breath and

nudged Top Hat into a trot.

Brian rode like a circus clown, a rein in each hand, both held high and wide. If he were conducting an orchestra, he'd have been doing double time. He laughed back at me, though, as if to say, "I'm doing it." *Dork.* I clamped a hand over my mouth so I wouldn't laugh out loud.

Old Charlie had the patience of a saint, but still, his ears were pinned back, and his head bobbed with each bounce Brian made in the saddle. Poor horse, he sent all the signals of his discomfort, tail swishing, head nodding, ears pinned back to someone who did not comprehend his language.

"Let's give Old Charlie a break." I walked Top Hat to a stream burbling down the hill, dismounted and held the reins while Top Hat drank.

"Why?" Brian dismounted, and Old Charlie drank, then swiped a bit at a tuft of grass.

"Old Charlie needs a break, and we need to talk about posting. It will help you keep your balance when we trot." The muscles in my neck stiffened.

Ms. Debbie always said, "Quiet hands are a rider's best friend." She was always patient and kind. I'd have to channel some of that patience now. Poor Charlie would suffer until Brian learned to post and keep his hand quiet, but could he learn all that before we got to Samson's? I reached into my backpack for my water bottle. Was I wasting my time?

I gasped. I lifted Mr. G's Smith & Wesson but didn't pull it out. A gun? When had he slipped it in my pack? A bag with five bullets rested on my hoodie in the pack.

"What is it?" Brian turned to stop Old Charlie as he nuzzled Top Hat.

"Nothing." I shook my head. Could I trust Brian? Would he be mature about it and not want to shoot it?

I couldn't tell him, not yet.

Brian let Old Charlie eat a tuft of grass. I lifted the flap and glanced at the revolver again. It was the one Mr. G had taught me to shoot last summer. The trails were dangerous, so Dad agreed to let him teach me. Did Mr. G think we'd need it? I glanced at Brian who patted the horse's head as though he were a dog. He used quick movements, and Old Charlie jerked his head away.

Mr. G used Top Hat for hunting, so he was used to gunshot, but was Old Charlie? He must have packed ammo too. I reached deeper, and my fingers found a box of bullets. Brian and Old Charlie had wandered down the trail, so I loaded the chambers of the revolver and clicked it shut, then flipped the safety on. I shoved it and the ammo toward the bottom, under my sweatshirt and my journal. Now we were ready, but for what?

I glanced at Brian. I had to tell him about the gun, but he'd want to be in charge, and he didn't even know how to sit a trot without falling off, let alone fire a weapon from horseback. I glared at him. *Ugh. What were we doing out here?*

I stared into the tangle of logs we'd have to circumnavigate. Stupid logs. They added precious time to our trip.

"We better hit the road." I avoided eye contact.

"Good. You can give me more riding tips, maybe?" Brian led Old Charlie to me and mounted.

I scanned the trail ahead. Sun dappled the trail, birdsong filled the air, and the rich aroma of earth churned by horse hooves filled my nostrils. The promise of spring unfolded the buds of vine maple, a sign of better times.

We jogged for a short time, and I glanced back to see Brian waving his arms around. He'd lost his stirrups and bounced a foot out of the saddle. Old Charlie pinned his ears back but trotted on. I let Brian catch up, and we trotted side by side.

"Time for another lesson. Look at Charlie's ears. See how pinned back they are? That means he's unhappy."

Brian stared at Charlie's ears but kept bouncing and waving his arms.

"Stop, stop, stop." I pulled Top Hat to a walk, and Charlie plowed into us. I grabbed his reins. "Geez, Brian." I frowned. "I'm going to teach you how to post."

"Post?"

"Stay here and watch." I nudged Top Hat into a trot and spoke over my shoulder. He frowned but listened. "I stand when I feel him bounce me, and I hold it as he takes a step, then I lower myself when he takes another step. I follow his rhythm, that way I'm not flopping around on his back or losing my stirrups, and I keep my elbows in and my hands still, over his withers." I turned and trotted back, posting. I watched Brian's expression.

He bit his lip. "I don't follow. Can you show me again?"

"Sure." I pulled Top Hat beside him. "Just do what I do. We'll go side by side, and when I say, 'up,' you stand. Then let yourself down. That's a post, like controlled bouncing, but don't drop into the saddle."

He shook his head and gathered Charlie's reins in his hands. I nudged Top Hat into a trot, and Charlie matched his pace. Brian's thigh rubbed against mine, but I ignored that. "Up—down—up—down. Feel the rhythm and move with it."

Brian rose and sat with each step, and soon Charlie's ears weren't pinned back anymore. I pulled Top Hat to a stop.

"Rest your hands low, right here on his withers, and pin your elbows close to your body. That way your arms won't flop around so much. Charlie will be happier if you post and so will your ass."

"My what?"

"You heard me. This is your first ride. We've barely left Mr. G's, and we have a long way to go."

Brian nodded as my words registered.

"Now try posting on your own. Trot down the trail and then back."

Brian nodded and took the reins. He held them without too much slack and tucked his elbows in. He placed them above Charlie's withers and nudged him into a trot.

"Up, down." I stood and sat as I said the words, and Brian caught the rhythm. He stood and sat with each of Old Charlie's steps.

"I got this. We'll be at Cedar Hills Farm in no time." He beamed.

I caught up to him. My favorite stretch of the trail was coming up, a long, loamy straightaway. Top Hat pulled at the bit and wanted to canter. Old Charlie would probably just trot faster, and Brian would lose his rhythm and either fall off or get saddle sores. It would be his first test.

I nudged Top Hat into a canter. Brian would just have to figure it out. But when I glanced back, Old Charlie was rolling along in a nice canter, and Brian had a smile that showed every tooth in his mouth. I glanced back at him and gave a nod. He had this.

The fir trees and logjams gave way to a stand of maple trees, several blown down and cleared from the trail. The standing trees had formed buds and would soon be covered in green.

"Look." Brian pointed down the trail.

I glimpsed a red metal barn with a white roof in the distance and pulled Top Hat to a stop where the trail forked at another logjam. Brian pulled Old Charlie to a stop beside me. We could still make out the roof of the barn through the budding foliage of Indian plum and vine maple growing up through the fir and maple trees left standing.

Mount Rainier rose in the distance beyond the destruction and mayhem that surrounded us, and Mount Tahoma stuck up like a middle finger. Mother Nature was flipping us off. I glanced at Brian. He sat Old Charlie like he'd been riding for years, not hours. The horse reached for a bite of salal, but Brian tightened the reins and stopped him like an old hand. He gazed down the trail where it forked, scratching his head.

"I'm not sure which trail leads to the barn, but this definitely reminds me of a Robert Frost poem." Top Hat fidgeted, and I held him steady. "It's one of my favorites."

"I think I know which one."

"You do?"

"Two trails forked in the woods, right? You're not the only one who reads poetry."

"Really?" I looked down my nose at him and raised my eyebrows. "Let's hear it."

"*Two roads forked in a yellow wood.*"

"Diverged." Top Hat sidestepped. "Whoa."

"Right. *Two roads diverged in a yellow wood,
and sorry I could not go both ways.*"

"Travel both."

"Good.
*And sorry I could not travel both
And be one traveler, long I stood
And looked down one as far as I could
To where it bent in the undergrowth.*"

He stared at the trail and pointed. "We are where the road diverges." His eyes twinkled in the dappled sunlight.

What was he waiting for? Praise? I nodded. "Okay, I'm impressed, but do you remember the end of the poem?"

He recited, "*I took the one less traveled by.*"

"*And that has made all the difference*," I finished. "So, which one do we take?"

Top Hat skittered sideways, and I nudged him forward through the narrow, overgrown trail. Old Charlie plodded along behind me.

"This one's the road less traveled by, but there's a gate, so someone still uses it." I rode to the gate and stopped, ready to put on another performance, but why did I want to impress Brian?

Old Charlie ran into Top Hat's rump, making him jump.

"Control him." I spun in the saddle and glared at Brian. "Do you want to get kicked?"

"No. I thought he'd stop." Brian shrugged.

"Top Hat and Charlie are friends, but you have to pay attention, or Charlie will get you both into trouble." I frowned at him. "Don't forget. You're the boss."

I tightened the reins, collecting Top Hat, and pressed

with my right calf. Top Hat reacted to my leg pressure and sidestepped to the gate. I opened it, Brian and Charlie rode through. I held the gate as Top Hat and I walked through, then we sidestepped the gate closed.

"That never gets old. Will you teach me how to do that?" Brian's smile caught me off guard.

I'd started out trying to impress him, but in the middle of closing the gate, my focus changed. I glanced away.

You don't care, remember? You can't afford to.

I cleared my throat. "That shouldn't be too hard. Charlie knows leg pressure. I'll teach you on the next gate."

Top Hat walked with a spring in his step. I had to hold him back. "What's your hurry, mister?" He never walked like this in the arena during lessons. Mr. G called his behavior "ring sour."

I had a lot in common with Top Hat, only I was "boy sour." How could I ever care about anyone when they disappeared from my life?

Don't go there.

I drew sweet air into my lungs, and Top Hat pranced sideways down the trail. What was he so excited about? I scanned the brush and trees. The barn loomed in the distance. Maybe he thought he was going to get fed?

My stomach rumbled. What was Mrs. Z doing right now? Probably worrying about us. If Mr. G could get his radio to work, maybe he would send her a message.

"I smell something." Brian held his hand over his nose.

Top Hat pranced, his neck high, ears forward. I gripped the reins and pulled up my bandana to cover my nose and mouth. It didn't help.

"Ugh. Something must have died." Brian pulled his shirt up to cover his nose too. "This barn's way bigger than Mr. G's."

"It's a dairy barn."

"How'd you know?" Brian shook his head.

"Mr. Coffey has over a hundred milk cows on this farm."

"How'd—" He shrugged.

"I have an uncle near Ferndale who raises dairy cows. He knows Mr. Coffey. My other uncle's farm is closer to Vandby. He raises goats and has a truck farm."

"A truck farm?"

"Yeah, veggies. My cousins help grow them. Maybe you've seen them at the market? They sell goat milk and cheese, too."

"Why didn't you keep your horse there?"

"On a goat farm?" I scoffed. "Dork—"

Oops. I clamped my mouth shut, but Brian's smile had disappeared.

"I mean—" Did I just do the thing I wasn't going to do?

Brian's face turned red.

I swallowed hard. "Sorry, you're not a dork. I-I didn't mean that." Wasn't this what I wanted, to hurt him? To stop him from liking me?

Brian held up a hand and rode past me toward the barn.

I shook my head. How could I be so stupid? I wasn't recovered enough to do this alone. I needed his help until we got home. I stared at his ramrod straight back. He was a dork, and so was I a little. Maybe he was into poetry?

"There's this poem by Emily Dickinson."

He ignored me, but I blundered on.

A WORD is dead
When it is said,
Some say.
I say it just
Begins to live
That day.

He nudged Old Charlie into a trot and bounced down the trail like a pro. I held Top Hat back, my stomach clenched, and my mouth dry. And just like that, he had shifted the power.

I nudged Top Hat into a trot.

Chapter Six

We skirted the pasture in a cold silence. Where were the cows? Mr. Coffey must have moved them to another field. Old Charlie refused to go directly across the field, and I couldn't blame him. The stench of death grew less potent as we rode out of the direct wind. We skirted the edge of the pasture, and as we drew near to the barn, I could see the house, with a cluster of trees running between the road and the house. There were chickens scratching in the yard, and tall weeds and grass filled the yard. Where was everyone? Was that the awful smell?

This was exactly why Mrs. Z didn't want us leaving the safety of Cedarville, and here I was with Brian, riding right into it. What was that old saying about not being able to predict the future? Humans must have made some colossal mistakes to bring down this much death and destruction on the world.

This was too similar to the Black Plague for comfort, one-third of the population had died from the plague. Did it smell like this? Why were my thoughts so morbid? I'd lost all the people I loved most, Grandpa Billy, Mom, Dad, and Shadow—

I shuddered. I couldn't lose anyone else. I glanced at Brian. Could I even afford to care? Was I going backward in the process of my grief? Shock and denial, stage one.

I stood in the stirrups, scanning the farm. "Brian…"

"Yeah?"

"This isn't Cedar Hills Farm."

"What? How do you know?"

"Mr. G said they had a red barn, but Cedar Hills Farm isn't written on this one's roof." I stared into the distance. The stench hung so strong in the air it made my eyes water.

****

We approached the house, the clop of horses' hooves echoing off the barn walls. Sweet alfalfa filled the air from the open barn doors. The hair on my arms stood on end. The farm seemed deserted. Whose farm was this?

Red, green, and yellow toys lay on the front grass. Something rustled under a bush, and Top Hat spooked, and Old Charlie's head jerked up, his ears pricked in the direction of the bush.

"It's a little kid." Brian dismounted and rushed to the bush before I could stop him.

He reached out his hand to the child. I couldn't make out what he said, but it must have been soothing. The grimy face of a little girl appeared from the bushes. Her curly, blonde hair hung in tangles, and her clothes were covered in dirt. Where were her parents? Brian picked her up, and she wrapped her arms around him, clinging with all her might. She was four or five, but what was she doing out here alone? I shivered.

Brian walked to me, and I shifted the backpack from my front to my back as Brian lifted the little girl to me without a word. I took her into my embrace and settled her in front of me in the saddle. She slumped against me, and a sour odor rose from her clothes. She lifted her big brown eyes to peruse my face, but didn't cry, smile, or speak. I glanced at Brian who shrugged.

I sighed, trying to push my own grief aside for this little girl who was all alone and hungry. We helped who we could, right? Mrs. Z had found me the week after Mom's funeral, bringing us another casserole, because who didn't need another casserole?

She found me alone and too sick to get to the bathroom. I couldn't stop her from moving into my house and caring for me, but no one would come for this girl, except for us. Her bony wrists hung from her coat sleeves, her hands cold as ice, but she didn't complain, didn't smile, didn't speak. I glanced at the watch, 12:16 a.m.

"What's your name?" I ran my hand over her tangles, but she didn't respond.

I stared at Brian's profile, strong and confident. I wanted some of that confidence if this was our new normal. He didn't suggest we check the house.

I hugged the little girl to me as I turned Top Hat and walked out to the road away from the house that reeked of death.

"Coffey farm must be close by."

"Agreed." My skin crawled. I wanted to get this little girl away from the smell of death. I nudged Top Hat, and we trotted down the driveway. A shiver shook her little frame. She raised her eyes to me once again, and I smiled, her body odors forgotten.

"I'm Olivia, and this is Top Hat." I patted his neck, and she reached down to finger Top Hat's mane. Had she ridden before? I pointed. "That's Brian and Old Charlie. Old Charlie loves kids like you."

"Do you like horses?" Brian asked.

The little girl nodded. He was drawing her out of fear. Would I have been able to do that?

"Do you have a horse?" Brian pulled up beside us and placed a hand on her shoulder.

She tensed, then went still and shook her head. We jogged the horses out of the yard and onto 96 without speaking. What was there to say?

****

We rode through fields of new spring grass. The birds flitted from branch to branch in the maple and alder that lined the road. Brian motioned with his head to a house off the road to our left. The girl pointed and stared. "Grandma."

"Is that your grandma's house?" Brian held Old Charlie's reins like I'd shown him, low and quiet. A warmth filled my middle. He had listened to me.

She shook her head yes, and her eyes glittered with tears, but her gaze never left the small white house. It sat in the middle of a tidy yard not too far off the road. There were no shrubs or trees, no places to hide.

"Shall we go see if your grandparents are home?"

She nodded, and I glanced at Brian. He steered Old Charlie in behind us, and we clomped down the driveway but only got halfway when an older woman stumbled onto the porch. She leaned heavily on the railing.

"Stop." She waved us off. "We're sick. Our well…"

"Grandma," the girl shrieked, and I clung to her so she wouldn't fall to the ground.

"Mary?" the woman cried. "Oh no. Honey, no. You can't come to Grandma's." Tears shone on her face. She held up a hand. "Grandpa's sick, and I…"

Mary squirmed in my arms, but I gripped her to my chest.

"I'm so sorry, baby," Mary's grandma wailed, "but it's for your own good."

Mary shrieked, "Grandma." She pushed against my arms as she struggled to get off Top Hat. "Grandma." She sobbed, her whole body shaking.

I tightened my hold on her.

"She's alone," Brian called, glancing from Mary to the grandmother. "There was no one with her when we found her."

"Oh my God. Ellie and Mack must be sick, or…" The old woman's voice trailed off. "Mary will die if she comes here." The woman stood on her porch, bent and gray. "Please take her to the Coffey farm. It's the next farm on 96."

"Yes." Brian nodded.

"Mary, you go with these nice people. You get to see Barb and Gracie. They will take care of you, honey." She pointed down the road.

Mary whimpered and squirmed in the saddle in front of me. Her little back arched as she pushed at my hands. I held her at the waist. She reached her tiny hand to her grandmother. A numbness ran through me, and my head began to spin. Why was this happening? The grandmother let out a choked cry.

"We'll take care of her." Brian waved to the grandmother. "We'll check in on our way back. The Coffeys might have medicine."

I gasped and shook my head at Brian. "We don't know if the Coffeys have medicine. Don't make promises you can't keep."

I hugged Mary as I fumed. Brian rode beside me, but he kept glancing back at the grandmother. My mind was racing. How long had Mary been alone? One day with that smell would be too long. I rubbed my chin on her hair, and the smell of ammonia hit me. Top Hat and Old Charlie picked up their pace as we rode away from Mary's grandmother.

Mary finally gave up her struggles and dozed in my lap, her clothes wet and filthy.

"Brian, what's the plan?"

"What do you mean?" He frowned.

"I mean, you know." I nodded to Mary.

"She's with us now." He glared at me daring to disagree.

He wore his commitment to Mary like a garment. This situation was black-and-white to him, and I shrank in my fears. He was right. She was one of us.

"We have to do this." He glanced at me. "We are the heroes of our own story, remember?"

I shook my head and stared at him. He nudged Old Charlie and trotted away from me, posting in perfect form.

Chapter Seven

The sun gleamed in a blue sky. It was still early, and the shadows were long. The only problem was I wasn't riding Shadow. I sighed. Finding Mary alone, dirty, and so thin unsettled me. Then her grandmother warned us not to come closer? Why did Brian's claim that Mary was "with us" affect me like this? He was the wannabe hero. I couldn't process it all.

Brian focused on the road ahead, scanning the pastures in the distance. The horses' hooves clip-clopped in a mesmerizing rhythm as we rode in silence. Mary must have been terrified being alone with her family in the house...

I held her to me as she dozed, a limp little girl curled in my arms.

Top Hat shied and danced across the road. Mary screamed.

"Hey." I fell back, then forward. Top Hat reared. I gathered the reins and clutched Mary to me, scolding myself. I should have been watching for things that would spook him. Old Charlie spun on his haunches, and Brian lost a stirrup but clung to the horse's neck.

I caught a whiff of cigarette smoke. Two guys stepped out of the underbrush onto the side of the road, passing a cigarette between them.

"Nice horses you got there. Give them to us."

I gasped. That voice. When had he started smoking?

Perry exhaled smoke. He was older and bigger than Brian. Aaron, his younger brother, was a sophomore like Brian but younger. He glared, then turned away, the stubble on his chin more like dirt than facial hair.

Perry. Didn't he recognize me?

I held Top Hat in check. Mary whined. Old Charlie stood in the middle of the road, his ears flicking back and forth. Brian patted Old Charlie's neck. "Easy, boy."

Perry leered at me. "Yeah. My feet are killing me since those bikes broke." He dropped the cigarette butt and ground it under his heel. Who was he now? Was this why he broke up with me, to run with Aaron?

The rumors of the Brewster brothers had been circulating since their mom died. "They are nothing but trouble," everyone said. Top Hat sidestepped as Aaron pulled out a knife.

"Horses might last longer than those cheap bikes." He rose to his feet.

I glanced at Brian. He ground his jaw and frowned, then gave an imperceptible nod.

He stood in his stirrups. "We're taking this little girl home. Why don't you go home?"

Aaron shook his head. He took a drag off his cigarette before flicking it to the side of the road. What was Perry thinking? He'd changed after his mom died, but stealing bikes and horses? This was getting ridiculous.

Should I call out to Perry and beg him to let us pass? He wouldn't hurt Mary, would he? Or me? We didn't have a relationship anymore, though. I nudged Top Hat, but he danced sideways, and Mary whimpered again.

"It's okay, Mary. Hang on tight." I glanced at the

time, 12:32.

Aaron rushed forward, his hand outstretched to grab Top Hat's rein. I held him in check but let him spin away. What a dumbass. He was going to get someone hurt.

I glanced at Brian. He shook his head.

"Run." I dug my heels into Top Hat, and he bolted past them. "Brian." If they caught him, they'd...

Old Charlie danced in a circle as Aaron lunged for him. I gripped the reins in one hand and Mary in the other as Top Hat raced down the road, adrenaline keeping me in the saddle. I glanced over my shoulder. I had to go back, but I had Mary. I hung on to Top Hat's mane and let him run. Mary twisted around and clung to me like a baby monkey. Top Hat raced around a bend in the road and hit the asphalt. He skidded around another corner. I sawed on the reins and slowed him to a walk, my breath coming in gasps and coughs. I turned in the saddle. Old Charlie hit the corner at a run, his ears flat back and Brian leaning over his neck.

Tears sprang to my eyes. "You made it." My hands shook as Old Charlie ran to us and did a sliding stop. Brian bounced two feet off the saddle. Top Hat sidestepped and circled, anxious and ready to charge again.

Brian released the saddle horn. "Are you okay?"

I nodded.

"Mary?"

She nodded.

"That was close." Brian met my gaze.

"Yes."

"The Brewsters are insane. I thought we were going to lose the horses. I mean—"

"But we didn't."

I glanced at him and nodded, trying to control my ragged breath. I nudged Top Hat into a walk, his sides heaving. "Those damn Brewsters."

"Language," Brian hissed.

I scowled. "We'd better keep moving before they catch us. Besides, we need to cool down the horses."

"Poor Charlie needs a ventilator." He patted Old Charlie's sweaty neck.

Mary reached up a dirty hand and brushed a tear from my cheek. I hugged her to me, and she snuggled into my arms.

Perry. What had happened to him? I'd never been frightened by him before, but now? He didn't remember what we'd had together.

"We'll be okay. Right, Mary?" I peered over my shoulder. "I don't think they'll catch us." My legs and arms still trembled as I adjusted my seat, and Mary settled against me. A wave of exhaustion crashed over me. "I guess Mr. G was right. They did take our bikes."

Brian furrowed his brow. "Something's wrong with those two."

****

The clip-clop of metal shoes echoed off the trees as we jogged down the road. Mary had nodded off again, her small form melding to mine. Brian held up a hand, and we stopped. Children's laughter rang out from behind a row of bushes.

Brian stood in his stirrups. "There's a house back there."

We came to a break in the bushes and stopped at the end of a long driveway. One of three kids spotted us and shouted to someone.

"Is this Cedar Hills Farm?" Brian waved at a tall

man in overalls. A woman in jeans and yellow sweater pointed in our direction, and the man waved. Top Hat nickered.

"Do you know this place?" I patted his shoulder. The red barn with a white roof came into view, Cedar Hills Farm painted in tall green letters on the metal barn doors.

"Yep, this is it." Brian trotted Old Charlie down the driveway, and Mary tensed in my arms as Top Hat tossed his head to loosen the reins. I ran a hand over Mary's matted hair.

Old Charlie reached the porch, and Top Hat joined him. Mrs. Coffey reached in her pocket and pulled out a carrot like this was a routine they had established.

Mr. G probably rode over occasionally? I would have done the same thing. Solitude is overrated sometimes.

"Hi. Mr. G sent us." Brian dismounted.

"I've been expecting him, not a couple of kids." He scratched his bald head. "I'm Samson, and this is my wife, Barb." He stared at Brian, then me, and frowned.

I slapped a smile on my face. "I'm Olivia, this is Brian—"

Brian cleared his throat. "And this is Mary. We found her at a farm down the road."

"Mary?" Barb gasped and rushed down the steps. She reached her arms to Mary. "Oh, honey." Mary threw herself into Barb's arms. Barb glanced at me. "Her grandparents," she mouthed over Mary's head.

I shook my head but didn't mention Aaron and Perry Brewster. Top Hat fidgeted, but Old Charlie stood with his head dropping and eyes closed.

"Someone needs a bath and some lunch." Barb

cradled Mary who clung to her. She raised her eyebrows at Samson.

"Thanks for bringing Mary. Barb will take care of that sweet girl." Samson seemed to soften, and his eyes twinkled as Barb carried the little girl into the house. The children trailed after her in a silent single file line.

A twinge of longing filled me. She'd be okay now, right? I shook my head to clear the memory of Grandpa Billy in Mom's arms.

"So, Mr. G needs that hay?" Samson picked up a toddler with curly brown hair. He scanned the barn and driveway as though looking for Mr. G.

"Yes." Brian sat taller in the saddle. "I'll help you deliver it and stay on to help him on the farm."

He was going to work for Mr. G? When had they decided that?

"That's good because he needs help. Why don't you two cool off those horses. I'll hitch up the wagon."

I patted Top Hat's neck. He was almost dry, but Old Charlie still had lather on his flanks. They did need a good cooldown.

Samson adjusted his toddler on his hip. "So, you two are heading back to Mr. G's with the hay?"

"That's the plan." I glanced at Brian who had dismounted.

Samson frowned. "Why didn't he just radio me?"

"It broke, and Angel is about to foal any minute."

"Angel. Right." Samson shook his head.

A child's cough came from the house, and Samson cleared his throat and gazed at the front door. "We have a sick one. Barb and I are worried."

"I'm sorry." I dismounted and walked Top Hat in a circle. He was acting like Mr. G before he asked us to ride over here.

The crying turned into a whine, and Samson winced.

"Brian can help me hitch up the team and load the hay, and then—" He paused and glanced at me from the corner of his eye. "—perhaps you could do us a favor?"

"Favor?"

"That's Gracie, our four-year-old. She's been sick for days and getting worse."

My stomach clenched. That was the look in his eyes. Fear. Did I have the strength to care? What if Gracie died too?

"She needs help we can't give her. I've been on the radio all morning with the clinic up at Franklin. They said the doc left for Yakima and won't get to Cedarville until next week, but they had an herbal mixture of some sort that worked. It's at the Franklin Health Clinic right on Main Street, and if we wanted, we could come get it." He paused. "Like I can leave my family."

I stared at him. He was desperate. That was all the glancing around and clearing his throat, but what about us? Was he insane? We were just kids. I had to get home to my birthday, right?

"It only takes a couple hours to ride to Franklin on horseback. You and Brian could ride up and be back by nightfall." He shifted the toddler on his hip. "You could save her life."

The little girl cried again. I shrugged. "I have to talk to Brian, and we'll have to let Mrs. Z know we're going, but..." I glanced at Grandpa Billy's watch, 12:44. I would miss my birthday party.

More raspy whines sounded from an upstairs room. Samson walked down the steps and grabbed my hand. He squeezed. "Thank you."

Wait. I hadn't agreed to anything yet. I stepped back.

"I'll send her a message before you leave. Gracie's our baby. That herbal medicine might save her liver and turn her around."

Had I just agreed to go? I had to correct him. Tell him I was still recovering, that I couldn't miss my party. My stomach churned as Barb's mumbled words of comfort filtered out an open window, and Samson pleaded with his eyes. He shuffled his feet.

Was it only this morning that I'd left in the hopes of finding Shadow? But I didn't find her, and Brian the Dorkmeister had shown up, and our bikes were stolen, then Mr. G, and Mary, and Mary's grandmother, and now Samson? I sighed. It went on and on, and everyone needed our help, but who was going to help us?

I gazed down the driveway as Brian lifted one of Samson's boys onto Old Charlie's back and led him down the driveway. A tightness filled my chest. He was ready to help, ready to load hay, and he'd be ready to save Gracie.

I came here to save the horses, and now I had to help Samson. I pulled my gaze from Brian and the laughing child on Old Charlie and nodded at Samson.

"I don't need to discuss anything with Brian. Of course, we'll ride to Franklin."

Chapter Eight

The horses grazed in the yard while Brian helped Samson hitch the team to the wagon and load it with hay. I stayed outside to watch the horses and keep Old Charlie from running back to Mr. G's barn. I rubbed Top Hat's neck and back with a towel Barb had given me. I glanced up to see her walking toward me across the grass. The delicious aroma hit me before she reached me.

She held out warm bread fresh from the oven, wrapped in a towel, and handed it to me with a smile. I opened the zipper on my backpack and placed it on top so it wouldn't get squished. This would make a nice dinner on our way back from Franklin with the medicine for Gracie.

As if on cue, Gracie wailed a plaintive call for Barb. I gritted my teeth. At least I was doing something to help. If we hurried, we could save Gracie. I slipped my arms through the straps and adjusted the backpack on my chest, then swung into the saddle. Samson and Brian strode across the yard.

"It's a straight shot up 96, so just follow the road."

The last sentence struck me like a slap in the face. 96 was not straight, and it was elevation, steep in places. Samson made it out to be a walk in the park.

He clasped Brian's hand and shook. "If Mr. G can spare you once you get back, I could use some help around here sometime too."

Brian beamed. "I'd like that."

Barb handed Old Charlie's reins to Brian. "What was that, hon?"

Samson shook his head, and she pressed her lips together. Was that a look? It definitely seemed like a look. Mom and Dad had "looks," code for something they didn't want us to know. Or was the look because he was hiring another hand they couldn't pay? A shiver ran down my spine. What would she say if she knew he was sending us into the mountains? Should I tell her? But I wanted to help. I wanted Gracie to live.

Barb patted Samson's shoulder. "Thanks for your assistance, Brian. This guy is not so young as he once was, no matter what he thinks." She chuckled.

"Watch it, wife." He put an arm around her and pulled her to his side. She smiled up at him, and he winked.

My chest constricted. They were so much like Mom and Dad. The hug, the kiss, the chuckles meant only for one another. Gone. I gathered Top Hat's reins, and he shifted, ready to go. Brian mounted Old Charlie, and Samson and Barb waved from the porch. As we rode down the driveway, I glanced at Grandpa Billy's watch, 1:37.

We were headed to Franklin. What could go wrong? The sunshine warmed my shoulders, and I scanned the green fields. In the distance, Mount Rainier sparkled in the April sun, the peak covered in clouds. Hmmm. Dad always said the mountain made its own weather.

****

Emma emerged from the kitchen, drying her hands. The cuckoo clock struck one thirty in the living room. It was her day off. Couldn't she get a moment's peace? She pulled the door open, and Josh gave her the smile he saved only for her. She stood on tiptoes and kissed him.

"Who is it?" Mom called from the dining room.

"Just Josh." She gazed into his eyes. It always made her tummy flutter.

Josh held her at arm's length and frowned. "Just Josh? Since when—"

She pecked him on the cheek, took him by the hand, and pulled him into the kitchen. "What's up? You're early."

He was early. "I just wanted to walk with you to the Johnsons'. Mom and Dad are arriving at two o'clock, and I thought we should arrive together since—"

She took his hand in hers. "Of course, we should. I can't wait to announce our promise to each other." It seemed all they did was meet at funerals. A wedding would be a nice change of pace.

Josh squeezed her fingers. He was terrified of losing her. She'd laughed when he'd begged her to quit working at the clinic. She dealt with sick and dying people every day. What would he do if—

He'd gotten on one knee and spoken his fears. "I don't want to spend these days worrying about you. Who knows how much time we have?" Not the most romantic proposal, but coming from Josh, it meant everything.

She'd quit laughing then but refused to quit working at the clinic. A pain formed in the pit of her stomach at the mention of death. Had she said yes only to ease his fears? She'd let him take her in his arms and kiss her, not that she'd ever minded that.

She pulled back and placed a hand on either side of his face. "I'll be ready soon. Mom is in the living room, ready to go. You can wait with her."

She waited until he'd disappeared into the living room, then she plastered a smile on her face and walked into the kitchen. She'd agreed to marry him because she loved him. Why couldn't she shake this anxiety over how much time they'd have together?

****

We let the horses set their own pace, which meant Old Charlie had to trot on occasion to match Top Hat's pace. Ten miles would take less than two hours with no stops or breaks, but could the horses maintain this speed? It would take three hours if we took breaks. We'd get the med—

"Look up ahead. What is that?"

I glanced at Brian. He'd looped the reins round the saddle horn and leaned back on his elbows on Old Charlie's rump.

"What are you doing?" I shook my head. "You're going to end up on the ground in two seconds if he spooks."

"Old Charlie wouldn't do that. He likes me." Old Charlie's bottom lip sagged.

Brian patted Old Charlie's neck.

"He's almost asleep."

"I am too." Brian gathered the reins. "We need some excitement. Can't we canter a bit? It would save us time and get us to Franklin faster."

"We need to pace ourselves, or Old Charlie won't make it. He's—well—old." I twisted in the saddle. Brian's mouth hung open ready to argue. "He already had to run from the Brewster brothers."

"That was fun. It felt like rolling waves."

"He can't run all the time, you know."

He pouted. *Dork*. I turned my head to hide my chuckle. "Okay, but just a short lesson on balance. I'll canter Top Hat, and Old Charlie should follow. Collect your reins like this." I tightened the reins and nudged Top Hat. "I'll stop at that log pile."

I clucked to Top Hat, and he cantered down the straight stretch of road. I glanced over my shoulder, and Old Charlie was rolling along with Brian clinging to the saddle horn, chuckling like a newbie. A tingle ran through me. His eyes sparkled. What had changed about him? I pulled Top Hat to a walk before we reached the logs. Old Charlie might try to jump one and hurt himself, or dump Brian.

He pulled up beside me, his hair windblown. "That wasn't very far." He patted Old Charlie's neck. The old horse puffed like Grandpa Billy after he'd climbed the stairs.

"We better look for a way around this pile."

A rustling in the salal made Top Hat spook. I tightened the reins in my hand.

I glanced at Old Charlie. He stood with his ears pricked, looking into the woods. I scanned the trees. I clutched the saddle as Top Hat danced. The bushes rustled. Top Hat snorted, and I held him steady with the reins. Oscar emerged, wagging his entire body.

"Oscar? OMG." I put a hand to my chest, my head spinning in relief that it wasn't the Brewsters. Top Hat snorted and sniffed in the dog's direction. Oscar was the last thing we needed right now.

"How did you find us?" Brian leapt off Old Charlie. Oscar ran to his open arms and licked his face, knocking him to the ground. Brian laughed, and Oscar jumped up and started running zoomies on the road.

"Don't encourage that stupid dog. I thought he was a bear."

Brian patted the dog's head. "Just be happy it wasn't the Brewsters."

I stared at him, shaken. He was right. They could be following us. I glared at Oscar who squirmed and bent himself in half, then zoomed to Brian again. "If you two are finished, we need to get to Franklin so we can get back to Gracie with the medicine, remember?"

"Right." Brian mounted Old Charlie as Oscar sniffed the pile of logs.

Oscar wagged his tail as he ran through the break in the trees. Maybe his being here was a good thing.

"Pfft." Who was I kidding?

****

The gentle incline of the road was easy here. I glanced at Brian. "Samson said we'd gain 1,800 feet over the ten miles to Franklin."

Brian patted Old Charlie on the neck. "How far have we gone?"

Dork. Was he enjoying the ride? I had to admit that I was too, so maybe that made me a dork.

"I'm not—" Top Hat tensed, and I scanned the road.

Old Charlie arched his neck, but Brian didn't seem to notice.

"Shh. Top Hat sees something. Pay attention." I cupped a hand to my ear, but all seemed quiet.

Charlie snorted and tossed his head to loosen the reins. The prancing palomino was spooked and getting ready to bolt, and Brian was clueless.

"Don't let him take the bit. Keep ahold of the reins and watch his ears. If they perk up and he stares in one direction, try to see what's spooking him. That way you're prepared and can calm him down." I held Top Hat steady. His whole body tensed as he stared at the forest. "A horse will spook at a plastic bag or a tree stump, and these two can sense something out there that is freaking them out."

"There's a lot of life in this old horse. He's so big and powerful." Brian ran his hand over Old Charlie's neck. Was he not listening to me? He didn't sense the danger he was in. Charlie's ears flicked backward, then forward. He snorted and lowered his head to release Brian's hold on him.

"Listen to—"

But Brian rode away.

Maybe it was a leaf blowing in the breeze that made the horses skittish. I secured my seat in the saddle. Oscar trotted around branches and trees in the road as we wound our way up into the mountains, the trees getting shorter and denser. With any luck, we'd get to Franklin, then back to Samson's. We still might make it home for some of the party.

We rounded a corner, but Oscar stopped and sniffed the air. He growled, and Old Charlie's head rose, his ears perked. Top Hat stopped, and all his muscles tensed.

Oh, crap.

I scanned the woods, holding Top Hat steady. Oscar growled and stared into the trees as Brian rode up beside me.

"What is it? Do you see something?" Old Charlie fidgeted, and Brian held the reins to steady the old horse.

"Quiet. There's something in the woods this time." I patted my leg. "Oscar," I hissed, but the dog ignored me. He crouched and growled.

Cigarette smoke wafted in the air, and I gasped. The

bushes rustled, and Aaron Brewster jumped into the road right before me. I froze. Oscar barked, and Old Charlie reared and spun. I grasped for his reins, but he was too quick. Aaron was closer and lunged for the horse, but Old Charlie squealed and leapt out of reach, with Brian clinging to the saddle as Old Charlie spun and danced.

Top Hat rose on his hind legs and pawed the air with his front hooves. I stood in the stirrups and leaned forward. Perry emerged from the brush.

"You can't have my girlfriend, dork." Perry shook his fist at Brian. "She'll never fall for a sophomore. You're way too young for her."

Top Hat scooted sideways. I gripped with my knees and held the reins tight. Was he jealous? What the heck?

Top Hat kept glancing at Old Charlie who reared with Brian clinging to his mane. Oscar growled at Perry.

"Ha, ha, ha. He can't handle that horse, and he's never going to get my girl." Perry put his hands on his hip and gazed in my direction.

"You—" I stared at Brian, my head spinning. Of course, they caught up to us. "Why are you following us?"

Perry ignored my question. "He can't have you. You're mine." He reached for Top Hat's reins. "We're taking you and the horse." He leered at me.

"I'm not yours, and I'm not going anywhere with you." I clenched my teeth, but Perry kept advancing, his eyes never leaving mine. Oscar crouched and exposed his fangs as he stood in front of Top Hat.

Old Charlie danced in a circle. Brian clung to the saddle horn with one hand and the reins with the other. He'd dropped one. I gasped. Hang on, Brian.

Aaron approached from the other direction, trying to

corner me and Top Hat, and Top Hat pulled at the bit and spun away. Oscar leapt at Aaron.

"Get her, Perry. We'll take her horse, then catch that palomino. Then we'll be able to find Pa." Aaron waved a switchblade in the air.

Where did he get that thing? Top Hat reared again, and I sawed on the reins. How long could I hold him? Oscar snorted, unsure who to protect, me or Brian.

"I've missed your pretty, dark curls, Oli." Perry squinted to protect his eyes from the smoke curling from the cigarette dangling from his lips.

Missed me? He hadn't missed me for one second, and where was his deadbeat dad? I glanced at Brian who glared at Perry. He should be grabbing that dropped rein. This could be a prob—

"I'll kill that dork and take his horse too."

Kill? I froze. I couldn't let him kill Brian. The gun, where was the gun? Perry and Aaron focused on Top Hat's flying legs as the horse kicked and reared. I held Top Hat's reins with one hand and reached into my backpack. I pulled out the gun in one fluid motion, pointing it at Perry.

Click.

I froze. "Crap." I glanced from Brian to Perry.

Perry shook his head. "Ha. It's not even loaded." Aaron took a step toward me, but Oscar lunged at him, barking.

I cocked the hammer and fired again, aiming at his feet. The explosion rang in my ears. Top Hat didn't flinch. Pebbles scattered on the road in front of Aaron, spraying his jeans. Oscar yipped and ran uphill. Old Charlie took the bit in his mouth and bolted downhill, with Brian clinging to the saddle. The sound of hooves echoed off the trees as Old Charlie ran for the barn.

"What the hell?" Aaron leapt backward. "You didn't say she had a gun."

"I didn't know." Perry dove into the brush, Aaron right behind him.

I kicked Top Hat who took off, but not after Old Charlie. He bolted uphill after Oscar like a shot, his stride long and steady. I no longer had the strength to stop him. *Hang on, Brian.*

Please don't let him fall off. Please. He'd be okay, right? He had to be okay.

Chapter Nine

Top Hat slowed to a trot and then a walk. He stopped at a pile of trees blocking the road. I glanced over my shoulder, but Brian was nowhere in sight. At least the Brewsters weren't following—yet. I uncurled my cramped fingers from the saddle horn, my sides heaving as hard as Top Hat's. With shaky legs, I dismounted and leaned against him, and he stumbled out of exhaustion. Oscar nudged my leg, and I patted his head.

"Where could Brian be?" My legs shook, and I clung to Top Hat with weak arms. He could have fallen off and broken a leg or an arm. A tremor ran through me. "I'm afraid."

Oscar nudged me again. "At least we have you on our side. You were awesome, Oscar."

I needed to go after Brian, but did that mean I didn't go to Franklin for the medicine? He would come after me until he found me. What's wrong with me?

I held a hand to my head. What did I do now? I never wanted to see Perry again, and going back after Brian might mean running into them. I buried my face in Top Hat's neck.

Go back, or go on?

I stared at the dark clouds gathering overhead. I might be closer to Franklin than Cedarville. I was alone, and I had to decide.

I knelt beside Oscar and pulled him into a hug. "What would Brian do?" Oscar panted and licked my face. "He'd go on, right?"

A tear ran down my cheek, and I brushed it away. Now was not the time to feel sorry for myself.

I picked my way around the logs, leading Top Hat. Oscar beat us to the other side of the pile, and we stared up the road. I'd just shot at Aaron, and I'd left Brian behind. Was this who I was now? Was this worth it? A tremor began between my shoulder blades and ran down my spine.

For the medicine, it had to be. I mounted Top Hat and nudged him with my heel. He turned to look at me.

"Don't judge. The Brewsters are back there, and I can't face them alone." I covered my face with my hands and swallowed my tears. "Besides, Old Charlie and Brian are probably halfway back to Mr. G's, and they'll bring help."

****

The world raced by in a blur, and Brian clung to the saddle horn. He felt like he was on a giant wave, rolling and rolling as Old Charlie pounded down the pavement. They hit a corner, and his hooves slid across the asphalt. He scrambled to catch himself, but Brian lost his grip and flew out of the saddle and into the brush.

He landed in a bramble of blackberry bushes, ripping his jacket and bruising his pride. He tried to untangle himself and grimaced, the thorns tearing his hands. He should never have let go of Old Charlie's mane, but he had no idea of how to slow him down. He replayed the fall in his mind. He'd thrown his arms up to balance himself instead of grabbing the reins. Stupid. Stupid. Stupid.

Olivia was right. He was a dork. He pulled the last vine from his pants leg and crawled from the bushes. He fell to the side of the road and lay on his side, wheezing like a beached walrus. Old Charlie did all the running, so why was he out of breath? The horse's hooves echoed in the distance until he rounded a corner, and all was silent. Old Charlie was going home.

Brian rolled over and rubbed his butt cheek. At least Olivia wasn't here. Would she have laughed? He didn't have to worry about that. He sat up and wiped the grit from his hands. Damn those Brewsters. He clenched his fists. He had to get back to her. What would Perry do if he caught her? Aaron said he'd take Top Hat. Would Perry stop Aaron from killing her to get the horse? He clenched his fists. He wouldn't let that happen, not as long as he was alive.

He rose to his feet and limped to the corner, peering around it. How far had Old Charlie run before he'd been thrown? Brian rubbed a hand across his forehead. He scanned the road but didn't recognize anything. At least the Brewsters were nowhere in sight.

Dark clouds formed overhead. He was sweating, but the temperature was dropping, and a tang in the air meant snow. He'd have to keep moving, or he'd freeze.

"I'm coming, O," he muttered.

Whether she wanted him to or not.

****

The trees at either side of the road created an alley funneling the breeze. I ran my hand over Top Hat's neck. It had finally dried. The last thing I needed was a horse with a chill. The sun grew weaker as it moved across the sky behind the cloud layer. I shivered.

"It's getting colder.

Oscar panted as he trotted in front of Top Hat.

"We'll have to keep moving to stay warm."

I glanced at the watch. 2:28.

I unzipped the backpack and reached my hand in the main compartment for my journal. I could write while it was still light. I fished around for the square corners, then pulled the zipper wide and gazed into the opening. Where was it? I poked my hand into every corner.

Had it fallen out when I grabbed the gun? I reached into the padded computer compartment, but it wasn't there. I dismounted and sat in the middle of the road and pulled out the entire contents. No journal. Oscar pushed his nose into my bag. I pushed his head away.

"No, no, no." I scanned the road behind us. It must have fallen out. That meant it was on the road where the Brewsters had attacked us, and I wasn't going to go backward.

Oscar sat beside me, and I pulled him to me. He was warm.

What if Perry found it and read it? "Oh no." I gasped. I'd written my deepest, darkest secrets, some of them about him. I covered my face with both hands. Oscar licked my cheek.

"Perry's reading my journal right now and laughing." Oscar licked my face again, knocking me over and falling into my lap, all seventy-five pounds of him.

Top Hat sniffed Oscar's head. I pushed the dog off and stood. He licked my hands and whined, wagging his whole body. What would I do alone in the mountains without these two?

I cleared my throat and pushed myself from the ground. "Thanks for the pep talk." Grabbing a stirrup, I swung my leg over and settled in the saddle. "We have to get to Franklin." I sighed.

Could I do this without him? I had to try.

****

The clouds boiled overhead. Was Brian okay? He had to be, and so did I. Oscar trotted ahead. I steered Top Hat around trees, trying to push the worry from my mind.

Stupid Perry. What did I ever see in him? Why couldn't he help us? Was it because of stupid Aaron? Since when did Perry listen to his younger brother?

Since his mom died. He got mean, but why didn't Brian get mean or destructive when his mom died? This was all Aaron's fault. A pain throbbed in my right temple, and I rubbed it.

"Shouldn't we be at Franklin by now?" I rode around piles of trees and debris that seemed to go on and on. Samson said we could get there and back before dark. Right. Maybe on a warm summer day, but this was spring, and spring in the mountains could be as deadly as winter.

Something lay in the road. I stopped Top Hat. Was it a pile of snow?

Snow would be bad, but it made sense. I wasn't prepared for this. I sniffed and wiped my nose with my sleeve. "If there's snow, maybe we're getting close to Franklin, right, Top Hat?" The wind blew through the trees from the west, and I shivered. "It's April. Shouldn't it be warmer?"

I stared at the corner where the road disappeared. "Samson lied to us so we'd go." Top Hat snorted. Did the horse understand me? He hung his head and plodded on. I patted his neck. "Are we crazy?" He swished his tail, and we continued into the mountains.

****

It was getting dark. Why was it getting dark? I dismounted and walked beside the horse. I blew on my frozen fingers. A branch snapped in the woods. I jumped and stared into the forest. Were the Brewsters following me?

"Franklin has to be around the next corner." I ran my hand under his mane, the warmth tantalizing to my fingers.

Top Hat snorted and rubbed my shoulder with his head. "I know. You need a break, but if we don't keep moving, we'll freeze." I leaned against his shoulder, warmth radiating off the horse.

"How did I end up headed to Franklin?" A gust blew through the tree boughs, and clouds billowed over our heads in vapors. It was cold enough to snow. That's all I needed. I shivered as a flake hit my cheek. Enough snow lay on the ground, thank you very much.

Mr. G could have ridden to Samson's for hay, but he'd refused to leave Angel. I got that. She could die without help and supervision. Maybe she was foaling this very minute.

I rubbed my fingers together. Samson should have ridden up here if it only took a day. Then I'd be headed home already instead of here alone. My stomach growled. What had people brought to the potluck, and why was I missing the first gathering that wasn't a funeral?

I held up my wrist, 2:56 p.m. I had to quit checking the time. I checked the dark clouds overhead. *I'm screwed.* How would I get to Franklin with more snow to contend with? I ran my fingers through Top Hat's mane. "We aren't going to make it, are we?" I sneezed, then coughed. Now what? The flu?

No. I was fine. I had to be. Who was I kidding? I was anything but fine. I walked a bit faster. Oscar glanced over his shoulder, then picked up his pace too. He enjoyed this trek up the mountains, stupid dog.

"Do you think the world will survive this?" My teeth chattered as we passed trees with snow still clinging to the branches. "I know you can't answer that, and I don't really want an answer."

Was I talking to a horse and a dog? Did it matter? They brought me comfort.

"I wish you could talk back." I sighed. "People survived pandemics before, like the Spanish flu. That was before penicillin and electricity. A lot of people died, but it wasn't the end of the world. We got this."

I rubbed my brow. Brian wasn't here, but I sounded just like the Dorkmeister. What did I care? I needed the sound of my own voice in this vast forest. "You're interested, right, Top Hat?" Top Hat turned his head to nuzzle my chest. Did he like the sound of my voice? "Then there was the Black Plague. People thought that was the end of the world. They didn't have science to explain what was happening. That was before antibiotics and stuff, but now without cars or airplanes, it seems like the Dark Ages all over again. If we could just get the doctor and her herbal mixture, maybe more people would live. If not…"

The fir trees rustled, and I wrapped my arms around my torso. "We are the survivors, and we'll be heroes, Top Hat."

Did I want to be a hero? That was Brian's thing. I wanted to help save people because I was tired of seeing them die. It left me hollow and helpless. I shivered. Right

now, I just wanted to be warm. Hot food would help.

Top Hat plodded up the road, his steps getting slower as the road grew steeper. I glanced at the sky. The clouds hung low and dark.

I held out my hand, and small flakes filled it.

"I sure could use a break right about now." Icy flakes hit my face, one after another, like frozen kisses.

I put my foot in the stirrup and mounted Top Hat. "We better find shelter, and soon. We won't survive long in the snow."

My thoughts whirled, and my shoulders tensed. A pain shot down my neck. We were going to die. Snowflakes fell, larger and faster. I nudged Top Hat into a jog, as Oscar jumped into the air, trying to catch snowflakes in his mouth. I swung my gaze left, then right, but the snow came down in larger and larger flakes.

The fir and cedar rose sixty feet above us, making it darker, but twilight gave enough light to expose a dirt road to the right. The snow brightened everything as it stuck. My hood was heavy with it. Oscar raced ahead, the snow flying off his back as he ran.

I reined Top Hat down a dirt road, the tree branches covered in snow, large flakes sticking as fast as they fell. Top Hat snorted and flicked his ears forward. What lie ahead, a cabin, the Brewsters? Top Hat shook his head, and snow flew everywhere.

Flakes the size of ping-pong balls fell, and an inch already covered the ground, muffling Top Hat's steps. We could die without shelter. I peered through the mesmerizing snow down the lane until my eyes ached. Brian was back at Silver Springs Stable. Mr. G was probably making supper.

We rode into a clearing, and a crude lean-to came into view. I slumped over Top Hat's neck in relief.

Chapter Ten

The clouds hung low in wisps, and the snow stuck, accumulating. My teeth chattered as I checked all six of the support posts. The roof would protect us from the snow, and the ground under it was dry, but without walls, we'd get the windchill. I dismounted and led Top Hat under the shelter. He snorted, sniffing the ground for something to eat. Oscar barked as snow swirled around us.

"It's definitely not the Deluxe, but it's protection from the storm." I kicked the dry dirt with the toe of my boot. At least we'd stay dry until the storm passed. I wrapped Top Hat's reins around a post and uncinched the saddle before pulling it off his back. I set it on the ground and sat my pack next to it, then checked the front pocket for the ten essentials. Dad wouldn't let us leave the house without them, and now it made sense. The matches alone would probably save my life.

The snowstorm settled over us like a white blanket. A stack of firewood sat at one end of the lean-to between two posts. A hatchet rested on top. I licked my lips and reached in my pack for water but hit the cold metal of the gun. I jerked my hand away. I never wanted to see that thing again. The sharp report from the shot still rang in my ears and made my stomach tie into knots.

I reached for the hatchet and began chopping off

slivers of kindling. I laid out kindling and small splinters of wood and lit it. It caught, and I fed small pieces, cutting more as I went. The wood snapped and crackled, and I added larger pieces until the fire blazed. The lean-to filled with a soft golden glow. Oscar chose a spot near the fire and circled a couple times before plopping to the ground with a grunt. Top Hat's eyes glinted in the firelight.

I blew on my cold fingers, then grabbed a small piece of wood from the pile and ran the block over Top Hat's back in a small circular motion, ruffling the hair, then smoothing it. He puckered his lip and reached his nose to the roof. "Is that your itchy spot?"

I brushed his back and neck until he was dry, then set the block of wood by the saddle. "You need water and hay." I scanned the area around the lean-to, fir and maple trees, salal and Oregon grape, but no grass. Spring came late to the mountains, so the weeds hadn't even started growing yet.

Top Hat sniffed my hands, his eyes filled with a wisdom and resignation I wasn't prepared for. Was he beyond caring? I wouldn't find anything for him to eat in a snowstorm. My teeth chattered. I didn't bring a coat, let alone gloves. Was this hypothermia? I was talking to Top Hat. Did that make me crazy?

I wiped my nose with the back of my hand. "Do you think Old Charlie and Brian are okay?" Top Hat lowered his head and began to nibble the dried weeds and grasses that weren't covered in snow.

"This day sucks." I reached into one of the bags and pulled out the bread Barb had wrapped in the towel. I closed my eyes as I tore a thick slice in half and stuffed a soft piece of the middle into my mouth. I fed Top Hat a piece of crust. Oscar's tail thumped on the ground, and I tossed him some crust. I shoved another piece into my mouth. Barb had packed four pieces, so I could eat one, share one, and save two for…

Say it. Brian. I wished he was here.

Did I? Dorkmeister? No. I scoffed, pushing that idea from my mind. I wasn't alone. I had a horse and a dog, and I'd be fine.

Oscar curled up beside the fire, and Top Hat cocked a hip. I laid out several pieces of wood so I could keep the fire going through the storm. Would it last long? I needed to keep going, one way or another.

I sank onto the saddle blanket, and with the strong aroma of damp horse tickling my nose, I curled up facing the fire. Grandpa Billy always loved a good fire. He would have been proud of me for this one. I reached out my fingers to warm them. Maybe the storm would end soon. I caressed the smooth face of Grandpa Billy's watch, 3:47. It was still early. If the snow let up, I could still make it.

My eyelids grew heavy as I stared into the flames. Maybe I wouldn't have nightmares tonight.

****

Josh held Emma's hand, and they walked up the steps. Emma's mom stood with them on the porch and beamed. Today was the day. Could he do it? He glanced down at Emma, and she squeezed his hand and returned his smile. Yes, he could.

He knocked on the Johnsons' front door. Tucker, the oldest of Dr. Johnson's sons, opened it. He waved them inside, his long legs covering the distance from the entry, living room, and dining room to the patio at the back of the house in seconds. He handed the bowl full of sauce to his twin Stevie.

"Hello to you two, Tucker, Stevie," Josh called, and Stevie held up the bowl in a mock toast.

The aroma of barbecued chicken embraced Josh like a hug. He scanned the room, stopping on the "Happy birthday Delores and Olivia" posters hung among all the bright decorations. Was there a Happy Engagement poster somewhere? A tingle ran through him.

Mom poked her head around the corner of the living room wall. "You made it." She pecked him on the cheek. "Carol." She took Emma's mom's arm and pulled her into the house and the gathering of neighbors. "I'm so glad we have something to celebrate for once. All we need is Olivia, and the party will be complete."

His pulse began to race. He gripped Emma's hand. Emma ran her hand up and down his arm. She could read his mind. He sighed. When would he get the chance to announce their engagement? Sure, they were young, but young people were dying.

Josh glanced over all the heads in the room looking for Olivia's dark hair. She'd better be here. A three-tiered cake sat on a table in the middle of the dining room, surrounded by cookies and tarts. Mrs. Z made it with real sugar. She'd begged and pleaded with every neighbor she had so she could create a masterpiece for Olivia, and she'd succeeded.

Two boys snuck a cookie from the table and ran out of the dining room and through the patio door, bumping into Stevie by the grill. Emma took his arm and chuckled. "Boys." She was still the feisty survivor he'd met during the storms.

"This is so good for Cedarville." Emma spun around, taking in the ceiling strung in streamers, the walls plastered in Happy Birthday Olivia and Delores and Congratulations Emma and Josh posters.

"Where is Olivia? She's missing her own party." She smiled up at him.

Warmth filled his chest. "She's just running late." He smiled as she took his hand, and a warmth filled his chest. He stared at his name with hers. This was really happening. He was going to marry Emma, and they'd be together as long as—

Mom led them to the tables heavy with food. He winked at Emma and squeezed her hand. She would be his wife in four months and sixteen days, but with the rise in illnesses and deaths, would they live that long?

He tried to ignore the dread, but still, the hair rose on the back of his neck. This party had to come up roses for Emma, without any disasters.

Please let Olivia arrive soon.

Mrs. Johnson bustled in from the patio. "There they are. Congratulations, you two." She gave Emma a hug. "The doctor and I are so happy. We haven't had cause to gather since—"

Mom held up a finger, and Mrs. Johnson snapped her mouth shut. Josh glanced at Mom and nodded. Did Mrs. Johnson almost jinx it? Mom had read his mind and stopped her. His jaw tightened. Nothing would ruin today. Nothing.

Cedarville deserved a celebration, delicious barbecue, lively music. He wanted this for Emma.

"Can we eat now?" Tucker put his arm around his mom's shoulder.

"I'm starving." Stevie joined the group.

Mrs. Johnson put her arms around each of their waists and gave a hug. They towered over her, their muscular arms clasped around her shoulder. "You boys are bottomless, I swear."

"Did you almost go dark, Ma? After our discussion?" Tucker frowned at her, but the glint in his eye gave him away. She shrugged and grinned.

Josh cast a quick glance at Emma. She winked at him, and he gave her a peck on the cheek. Mrs. Johnson sighed.

Were they on display? So be it. He pulled his bright, intelligent, future partner to his side.

A light breeze blew through the patio door, through the living room, dining room, and out the front door. It brought the bite of winter to hang in the house. Where did that come from? It was mild with the promise of spring only this morning.

Mrs. Z joined the small group, and she was frowning. Josh braced himself.

"Olivia and Brian aren't here yet, and the temperature is dropping." Mrs. Z wrung her hands. "I told her she couldn't ride her bike to Mr. G's, not on the day of her party, but you know Olivia. I even sent Brian to make sure she got back in time." She gestured to the air. "Where are they?"

This can't be happening. Josh located his father in the crowded room and crossed his fingers that Olivia and Brian would walk in the door.

"Not home?" Mom frowned.

How could he head off this disaster?

Emma placed a hand on Mrs. Z's arm. "I thought Olivia went to Mr. G's? Maybe Tucker could radio him."

Josh placed his hand on Emma's shoulder. She was in her save-the-world mode. *I'm going to wring Brian's neck when I see him.*

Mrs. Z dabbed at her eyes. "She's been pining for that horse since Mr. G sent the message about colic. She thought she could scheme to go to the barn behind my back, but her emotions are transparent, but I thought Brian could talk some sense into her."

"Tucker has sent several radio transmissions to Mr. G, but we couldn't reach him, right, son?" Mrs. Johnson's pride shone from her eyes as she spoke.

The party was spiraling out of his control. Josh opened his mouth, but Mom interrupted him.

"Ed needs to know if he doesn't already. It's supposed to snow in the mountains." Mom pushed through the crowd across the room to Dad who was piling potato salad on his plate and laughing about something with Virg Taylor.

Josh watched the scene unfold as if in slow motion, Mom reached his side, spoke in hushed tones, and he put his plate on the table. They returned, Mom whispering in his ear.

Josh braced himself as Emma stood poised for action. She'd want to be at the clinic in case they needed medical care. There would be no stopping her once the alarm bell was rung, and Dad was about to ring it. He loved her ability to take charge without fear. He loved that if she could help someone, she would, but his one goal to save this celebration had failed. It was all over except the forming of a rescue team.

Dad stopped in front of Mrs. Z. "What's this about Brian and Olivia not back yet?"

She nodded her head, her short white hair perfectly coifed.

"But I thought they were going to Mr. G's, then coming right back?"

Josh sighed. The new normal was to keep track of everyone, and this was why. So they could save each other, and this time, it was Olivia's and Brian's turn. The whole town would join in the rescue.

Mr. Grady burst through the front door and scanned the room.

Right on cue. Josh couldn't stop this train wreck if he tried.

Mr. G wiped his brow. Had he run all the way from his farm? His hair was disheveled and his breathing ragged. He approached the circle of people surrounding Emma.

Mrs. Z rushed to him. "Where are my kids?"

He scrunched his hat in his hands. "Old Charlie came home in a lather."

"What?" Mrs. Z wrung her hands.

"My stupid radio—I knew you'd all be here, so—"

"Slow down." Dad put a hand on Mr. G's shoulder. "What does Old Charlie have to do with this?"

Mr. G ran a hand over his thin hair. "They were doing me a favor. They went to Cedar Hills Farm to tell Samson I needed that hay, but they never came back."

"What are you talking about? They left here on bikes." Mrs. Z glared at Mr. G.

"I know, but the bikes were stolen, so they had to go on horseback, Brian on Old Charlie and Olivia on Top Hat, but Old Charlie came running into the yard—" He glanced at his watch. "—an hour and twenty minutes ago, and I haven't seen any sign of Brian or Olivia. They are still out there somewhere."

"If Old Charlie returned, then Brian must have fallen off." Mrs. Z glared at Mr. G. "What were you thinking, you old fool?"

"My horses are starving, is what I was thinking. Samson said he'd help, but my radio—" Mr. G wiped his brow. The sparks of anger flew between them as Mrs. Z dragged the information out of the older man.

"If you mention that radio—" Mrs. Z growled.

Emma gasped. "Samson? Oh no." She put a hand to her mouth. "His youngest, Gracie, has been sick."

"Gracie?" Josh tightened his grip on Emma's shoulder. She put her hand on his. Samson would do anything to save his kids. "You don't think—"

"It's his little Gracie." Emma nodded. "That's exactly what I think."

"Will someone tell me what's going on? I'm so worried." Mrs. Z's fierce gaze shot from Mr. G to Emma. "Tell me," she whispered.

"First, there's a snowstorm in the mountains." Dad reached for Mrs. Z's hand, and she let him take it. "Second, if Gracie's sick, Samson might have talked them into riding to Franklin to get the medicine we've been waiting for."

Emma nodded. "Dr. Nordby got stuck in Yakima and couldn't bring it last week as scheduled."

"I don't understand. Why would Samson ask them to go?" Mrs. Z's face sagged as Emma's words became clear to her. "They're just kids. This is your fault, Mr. Gill Grady. Why did you send them to Samson's?"

Mr. G stared at his shoes. "I was desperate. I couldn't leave because Angel hadn't foaled yet. I—"

"And we're just finding this out now?" Dad sighed. "Were Olivia and Brian dressed for snow?"

"No," Mrs. Z wailed.

Mr. G cringed. "I came as soon as I bedded Old Charlie down, and checked on Angel and her foal, a little filly—"

Mrs. Z shook her fist at Mr. G. "You bedded down Old Charlie and checked on Angel? What about those kids?" Mrs. Z stomped her foot.

Dad tapped a finger on his chin. "We better assemble the rescue team. Virg?" He glanced at his watch. "It's almost four o'clock. We'll have to hurry. They can't have gotten far. We might be able to reach them today."

"Why would Samson send them? Did he think they could get to Franklin and back in a day?" Mrs. Z wrung her hands. "I could ki—" She unclenched her fists. "I'm sorry." She glanced at Emma. "How is poor little Gracie?"

"I was out there yesterday with Dr. Johnson. She is one sick kid, and they don't have running wa—"

Mrs. Z's shoulders slumped, and she shrugged. "I know. I know. I can't believe that this is happening. It's like living in the Dark Ages."

"It all comes down to water." Mr. G scrunched his hat in his hands. "We used to turn the tap, and it rushed out. Now it makes us sick."

Josh put a hand on his shoulder. "Without water from the tap, we are all at risk of disease." He glanced at Emma. Her face glowed, even as their celebration went up in smoke. Her dedication to this town was one more thing he loved her for.

He stepped forward. "This might not be the right time, but more workshops on proper latrine installation will help curb the spread of disease."

Mrs. Z put a hand to her chest. "That's right. Too many people are just digging holes in the ground and contaminating the water. So many people are d—" Mrs.

Z stopped, her eyes red and watery. "I'm so worried. Olivia and Brian are like grandchildren to me. I don't know what I—" She broke down, her face in her hands.

The party was over. Josh cleared his throat. "We'll find them, Mrs. Z."

"We will." Dad ran his fingers through his hair. "I'm sorry, Mrs. Johnson, but we're going to have to disband the party and form a rescue team. We'll leave ASAP."

Dad gazed into the distance, the wheels of his mind turning.

Josh pulled Emma to him, and she leaned into him, wrapping her arms around his waist. Her calm acceptance pacified him. They had the rest of their lives to celebrate birthdays and engagements, but right now, Olivia and Brian needed help.

Chapter Eleven

I pulled the saddle blanket tighter around my shoulders. The wind blew snow into the shelter. Each flake sizzled in the flames. Was that what woke me? Ugh. Still snowing, still cold. When would it stop? I grunted as I reached for a piece of wood to lay on the flames.

Footsteps approached from the road. I froze.

"Want some help with that?"

I grasped a piece of kindling and jumped to my feet, waving it over my head like a weapon. Was it Perry? I gripped the piece of wood like a weapon, staring into the snow. Why hadn't I put the gun where I could reach it?

The man stood drenched and shivering at the edge of the lean-to. "Watch it with that thing." His teeth chattered, so I could barely make out his words.

"Brian?"

I dropped the wood and flew into his arms. He wrapped his frozen arms around me and held me tight, his whole body shivering. I pulled away.

"You followed me. I mean—" I stared into his eyes and leaned into his quaking body.

His lips were on mine before I could stop him, but they were warm and soft, and I clung to him. He shivered, and I pulled his wet body to me, trying to warm him. He pulled away, and I opened my eyes.

"Does this mean you're actually happy to see me?" He grinned, and Oscar nosed in between us. I took a step back.

"Happy?" I stared at him. "What?"

Dorkmeister. He had hypothermia.

Heat rose from my neck into my cheeks. "I thought you and Charlie…" I shook my head. "Gah. I was worried sick about you, and that's all you have to say?" I pulled him to the fire and wrapped him in the blanket. Was he delirious?

"Mmm." He pulled the blanket over his head and leaned toward the fire.

I frowned at him. He'd kissed me, and I let him? My stomach tingled, and I cleared my throat. Snow surrounded the lean-to, and the heat from the fire radiated. Brian held his shaky hands out to the flames.

"You're freezing. Are you crazy?" Was I mad at him? He could have died trying to find me.

"I'm just wet and tired." He shook snow from his hair. He was drenched.

"I'll build up the fire."

For once, he didn't argue, and I stirred the embers, laying on small pieces of wood. They caught, and I reached for my pack. "Hungry?"

He nodded. "I could eat a…"

"Don't say 'horse.' Apologize to Top Hat this instant."

He chuckled. "Sorry, Top Hat." Oscar sat up, licking his lips.

I unwrapped Barb's bread and handed him a slice. Brian took a bite of the bread and chewed. I stared into the flames as Brian chewed the bread. I had never been truly alone. Brian had been right behind me—but that meant the Brewsters might be too?

"You weren't followed, were you?"

"I was on the lookout for the Brewsters, if that's what you mean." Brian pulled out his canteen and drank. He gazed into the fire.

Was he thinking about Perry's angry outburst? "She's mine. You can't have her."

I hated Perry. Why would he say such a thing? I shook my head. "I don't know what I ever saw in Perry."

Brian ignored my comment. "I stayed off the road, after Old Charlie threw me."

I wiped my nose on the back of my hand. "But Old Charlie got away?"

"I think so. I reached the spot where they'd attacked us, and there was no sign of them, so I'm pretty sure the gun scared them away. They know we have a weapon, so they won't follow us." He took another bite and chewed.

"I can't believe you found me."

"I would never leave you. I followed the road, then the smell of smoke. We must be the only people stupid enough to be up here." He took another bite and chewed as he stared into the fire.

"If you found me, so can the Brewsters." I stared into the flames. I bit my thumbnail. "Why didn't you just ride Charlie back to Samson's?"

"I fell off, remember? Charlie was long gone before I could climb out of the blackberry bushes. Besides, I figured I was closer to you than Samson's, so I decided I'd just catch up with you, and here I am."

I didn't know whether to believe him, hug him again, or scold him for being an idiot.

He hung his head. "I think it's going to take both of

us to get to Franklin, and I wouldn't be able to live with myself if—"

"You're exhausted." I couldn't let him finish any statement that ended with the word *die*. "Rest while you can. We can't leave until the storm subsides anyway." I patted his shoulder.

Steam rose from his clothes.

A wind blew through the lean-to, and I scanned the area for a tarp or anything to create a windbreak. "We need to warm your core."

"We could share body heat."

"What?" I shook my head and clamped my mouth closed. Was he serious?

"I'm drenched. We're both freezing, and we'll both get hypothermia if we don't figure this out." His teeth chattered.

He was right. Shared body heat would save us both. He stared into the flames. Why had he followed me? Heat rose into my cheeks.

"We are doing this to survive and nothing else. Right?"

"Right." He yawned and curled up next to the fire.

I laid down beside him, surprised by his warmth.

****

I shot bolt upright. The fire snapped and crackled. I scanned the horse blanket, the fire, the snow a foot deep just beyond the lean-to roof. Where was I?

I rubbed my eyes, my dream receding. Brian sat beside me, warmth radiating from him. He leaned over to push hair from my face. I froze. We were in the mountains, in a snowstorm, and sleeping beside a fire to survive. Then why was my heart racing?

He frowned. "You look like you've seen a ghost."

"What?" I glanced at his full lips and turned my face away, heat rising into my cheeks. "No, I'm fine."

He was too close. Why didn't he get up? I turned to face him, and he leaned over. Why didn't I get up? He pressed his lips to mine. I couldn't move. I settled in his arms, and the warmth we shared soothed me. He pressed his lips against mine harder, and I responded. Oscar nudged my leg, and I jumped to my feet.

What just happened?

I stumbled to Top Hat, the cold air shocking me. I rubbed my fingers around his eyes, and he grunted with pleasure. I glanced back at Brian as Oscar stole my warm spot, and a flush rose to my cheeks. I buried my face in Top Hat's neck.

"There's no latrine, so…"

I glared at him. Was that all he had to say?

Would I be happier if I were alone? I touched my lips and frowned. Had I just kissed the Dorkmeister and liked it? I shuddered. He grated on every nerve I had. I checked the watch, 4:19.

"Look. I'm glad you're here, but we have to keep moving. We can't spend two more minutes in—"

"You're right. It's too exposed." He ran his fingers through his thick hair that stood out in cowlicks all over his head. "We have to get to Franklin."

I clamped my mouth shut before I said, "Thanks for stating the obvious." Instead, I said, "We need to find water for Top Hat as soon as I get back." I stomped into the bushes.

That didn't sound bossy at all. I peeked over my shoulder, but Brian ignored me. Sure, he'd kissed me, but if he thought he was going to ride on Top Hat with me…

I rushed back to the fire and found him pouring water into his hand and Top Hat licking it off. He'd rummaged through my backpack. I bristled, but it contained both of our stuff, so he was entitled. I blew out a steam cloud, releasing tension with it.

He hung his head, and his voice came to me quiet as a caress. "I'm sorry I lost Old Charlie. It'll take us longer to get to Franklin now."

"It's no one's fault." My eyes itched from unshed tears.

I clenched my fists. He was right. It would take longer. "We have to stay here tonight."

He nodded. So far, this journey sucked.

Chapter Twelve

Emma squeezed Josh's hand. His tension made her nervous. When would he learn this world wasn't perfect? Perfect was for sissies anyway. So what if the Johnsons' party turned from celebration to rescue mission planning session? Emma didn't mind.

This was supposed to be Olivia's birthday party too. Emma needed to help find her. Poor Gracie, she was at the center of it all, sweet little girl. She must be really sick for Samson to send Olivia and Brian into the mountains. Did he not know about the snowstorm? Dr. Woolf would have some strong words for that guy, sick kid or no.

Dr. Woolf had drawn a map, and he'd distributed the lists of supplies each one of them were to bring for the mission.

"It's too late to leave today," Dr. Woolf said. "Let's meet at the clinic at seven o'clock tomorrow morning. We'll need all the daylight we can get."

Josh sighed. "This isn't what I had planned for today."

"I know." She smiled at him and brushed the hair that had fallen over his forehead and into his eyes. "You can make up for it with a stroll through the park."

He chuckled and took her hand. "Done."

She pulled him out the door, but her mind returned

to Olivia and Brian. They'd better be okay, or Samson was in big trouble.

****

Shared body warmth, who knew I'd need that, but right now it wasn't enough. "Brian. Brian." I waited.

"Hum?" Brian stretched and opened his eyes.

"Are you asleep?"

"Not anymore. What's up?"

I shivered. He pulled me to him, and I sighed. His warmth was delicious. "Listen. I think we have to leave. This lean-to doesn't provide enough shelter."

"Are you crazy? It's still dark." He rubbed my back and arms.

My teeth chattered. "I can't sleep. I think we should pack up and go. Maybe we'll find a cabin. All I know is I can't stay here. I'm too cold."

"Okay. By the time we're ready to leave, it might be a little lighter." He pushed himself up on an elbow. "If we are going to do this, we better pack quickly and start hiking to stay warm. Maybe Top Hat will share his heat?"

"Poor horse. He didn't sign up for this. We volun-told him. It might be good to get his blood flowing too."

Snow pelted Brian's face with each gust. "Great. Snow and freezing temps."

"We are in the mountains." I tried to grin, but it took too much effort.

He brushed the flakes away and rubbed his eyes as he shook out the saddle blanket.

****

Brian walked on one side of Top Hat, his hand on his hip, and Olivia rode. The horse stumbled. Light penetrated the thick cloud cover, but it was a dim gray light at best.

He couldn't stop staring as her hips swayed with each step of the horse. He'd kissed her, and she kissed him back, right? It didn't mean anything to her. Let it go.

Top Hat swished his tail, and Brian glanced at his ears. They were forward, so he wasn't angry. Her body moved as one with the horse. She nudged the horse into a slow jog.

Man. She wanted to get away from him. He'd blown it. So, what if he was a sophomore and she was a junior? He'd never met a girl like Olivia. He'd tried to forget her when she started dating Perry, and he became invisible.

Perry was history, though, and he had her alone, and what was the first thing he did? He shook his head. Why did he kiss her? Because it was so natural to pull her to him, and it seemed like she wanted him to kiss her. He stared after her slender form on the horse and shook his head. He'd kissed her, and he didn't regret it.

She'd kissed him back, hadn't she? Yes. She had, but then she'd frowned and pushed him away. Girls.

He sighed. She was a junior, but he would be too if it weren't for El Primo. He was two months younger than she was. His parents and teachers had started the process of moving him up a grade when El Primo hit.

Would that have made any difference? She was only here to get medicine for Gracie and Cedarville, and he should focus on that too. Everyone depended on them. He wiped his nose on his sleeve. Was he up for this challenge? Was she?

Oscar ran back to him. Brian ruffled the shaggy mop of hair on Oscar's head before the dog crashed into the underbrush after an unseen squirrel. Brian shook his head.

I'm overthinking this. She's made her feelings clear. Focus on getting the medicine.

****

Oscar popped out of the bushes and bounded down the road. Brian jogged to keep up. It kept him warm, but he couldn't go on like this forever. Why was she always angry?

Dude, she doesn't like you, remember?

No. She didn't like him, but he couldn't stay away. Why did he follow her? Mrs. Z had encouraged him, but that was when the plan was to go to the barn and back. Now they were halfway to Franklin in a snowstorm. This was his fault. He was the one who'd wanted to help Mr. G.

Why didn't he stop her when she agreed to go? Then Samson talked them into going to Franklin. He wanted to help, but Olivia was still recovering from her own bout of illness, and she grew weaker by the minute. Samson was more concerned about Gracie, of course. He'd do anything to save her, but at whose expense? Theirs. Olivia was riding through a blizzard, and the Brewsters…

He sighed. Perry. It was useless. He gripped his once-chubby fingers into lean fists. How much weight had he lost since his illness?

She'd never like him. But she had kissed him back, twice.

He shook his head. They had to get the doctor if they were going to save Gracie and all the folks in Cedarville, right? The problem was he didn't have a horse to ride.

He shuddered. "Old Charlie."

Chapter Thirteen

Snow hit my face, and I wiped my eyes and shivered. Had I dozed in the saddle? Where was I? I rubbed my face and yawned. Brian walked beside Top Hat. That's right, the kiss. I put a hand to my lips and pulled it away, heat rising into my cheeks. Just act natural.

What was natural at this point? We were on our way to Franklin to pick up the tincture that would save Gracie, but now we were caught in a blizzard.

"I'm surprised you didn't fall off."

Brian the comedian. Great.

I rolled my shoulders to work out the kink in my neck. My teeth chattered. "Why is it still snowing? How long was I out?" I glanced at the watch.

"I don't know, a while, but the snow never stopped. It's six inches deep now." He stomped his feet.

"You must be freezing."

"I'm fine." He blew on his fingers.

"We should have stayed at the lean-to." I wiggled my numb toes.

"No. The breeze blew right through that place. We never would have warmed up."

I sighed and stretched, then pulled my hoodie tight under my chin. "Where's that stupid dog?" My whole body ached.

The underbrush rustled, and Top Hat's ears flicked at the noise. Oscar pushed his way onto the road and to Brian's side. Top Hat snorted, and Brian ruffled the dog's hair. Did he even remember the kiss?

My stomach growled. Hunger would take my mind off him. I held up my wrist. The watch read 6:07. I frowned. How had my trip to see Shadow turn into this Odyssey? My teeth chattered.

Brian brushed snow off his shoulders. "We have to get to Franklin today before dark and my feet are frozen solid. Damn this snow. It makes walking impossible."

"You're right." I stared at the snowflakes, drifting rather than falling. Maybe it would stop soon? It had to. It was April. I sighed. I didn't have the energy for this. I stared into the distance. Was this how it started?

Hypothermia.

I brushed snow off Top Hat's mane. "There's food in Franklin, right?"

"Fresh bread and hot soup, last I heard." Brian chuckled and coughed.

I shivered. The last thing we needed was to get sick out here. "Fresh bread. Mmm."

How did we get talked into this? The snow came down in larger flakes, and the wind pierced my jacket. I shivered again and glanced at Brian. We had to get to Franklin, not only for the town's sake, but for our own.

****

We plodded on like zombies. The snow had stopped, but it lay in deep drifts over the road. The trees were thick with snowy branches. A high-pitched squeal rang through the forest, and Top Hat's head flew up. He pointed his ears toward the sound. Oscar stared into the trees, and Brian grabbed him by the collar.

He'd followed me. Was I happy about that? I was happy he was okay but confused about the kiss. I'd never make it to Franklin without him.

Oscar whined, and Brian tightened his grip. "No. You don't get to chase the elk."

"That was elk? Sounded like—I don't know what that sounded like, a squeaky door hinge?"

"It was probably a cow elk warning off another cow. The pregnant ones are calving." He scratched his head and gazed in the direction of the bugle call. "It came from downhill about a half mile away, I'd guess."

"How do you figure that?"

He shrugged. "A hike I took with my…" He stared at his hands.

I shuffled my feet. "Sorry." Did I just remind him of his dad? That wasn't awkward at all. I patted Top Hat's neck, then reached a hand to Brian, and he swung up behind me.

He wasn't so bad. At least he kept me warm. A tingle ran through my belly.

Oscar raced down the road. Another bugle call rang through the air, but this one sounded muffled. "Do elk attack humans? I heard a story one time—"

"We're leaving them behind, so it doesn't matter."

"Right." I leaned into Brian's body warmth, and he rested his chin on my shoulder. I wanted to push him away, but the warmth was too enticing to resist. That was my excuse anyway. Oscar trotted ahead, his tail wagging like a flag.

"It's like he knows the way?" I turned to glance at Brian.

"Maybe he smells lunch cooking." He chuckled. "Lead on, brave explorer, and we shall feast upon our arrival."

"Pffft." I didn't want to encourage his dorkiness, but I did want dinner.

****

Emma tossed and turned all night long, her dream of a funeral and a snowstorm with quicksand that sucked her under until she couldn't breathe startled her awake. The cuckoo clock struck seven o'clock. She swung her legs out of bed and stepped into a pair of jeans. She slipped on a T-shirt and grabbed a hoodie from her closet.

Would she be able to hold her anger in when she confronted Samson? She clenched her teeth as she buttered toast.

"Coffee?" Her mom handed her mug. "Who's on your list for slaying today?"

"What?" Emma took a bite of bread, and her mom tucked stray hairs behind her ear.

"You look like you're going to war, not to help Gracie."

"Mom. I already told you what Samson did." She sipped the coffee and sighed.

A knock came from the front door.

"It's Josh and his dad. Bye, Mom." Emma kissed Mom's cheek and guzzled down the coffee. "Hot. But it might be the last cup I get all day."

"Be careful." Mom walked out of the kitchen behind her, wiping her hands on a dish towel. "You too guys. You all take care." She waved at Josh and his dad, as Emma pulled the door closed behind her.

They turned right on Second Street, walked two blocks, turned left on Salmon, and then made their way the final three blocks to the clinic. Dr. Johnson shouldered his pack of medical supplies. His sons, Tucker and Stevie, shoved and wrestled in the street in front of the clinic.

"Act your age, guys." Dr. Johnson frowned at his sons, his blue eyes hidden under his bushy brows.

"We are." Tucker and Stevie replied in unison. Tucker shook his blond head.

"Well, act older than seventeen, then." Dr. Johnson tried to hide the smile growing on his face. He nodded at Emma, and she shouldered her bag.

She often accompanied Dr. Johnson on his home visits, but this time was different. If Samson really sent Olivia and Brian into the mountains, she was going to give him a piece of her mind, then wring his neck.

Dr. Woolf held up his index finger and made several circles in the air. "Gather round, people."

Josh took her hand, and Emma wanted to kiss him, but this was a rescue mission.

"We'll head to Virg's place at the edge of town, then he'll drive us to Cedar Hills Farm. We'll drop off Dr. Johnson and Emma and proceed up the mountain. With any luck, we'll find Olivia and Brian this afternoon and be back in Cedarville before nightfall. Should be an uneventful trip. Okay?"

"Famous last words." Stevie shoved his hands in his pocket.

Dr. Woolf cocked an eyebrow. "Don't jinx it." He scanned the group of six people and nodded. "Right, then. Next stop, Virg's."

Emma and Josh brought up the rear of the procession as they left the clinic and headed to Virg's small farm on Branch Street near Highway 96 and the edge of Cedarville. They tromped uphill, and Emma's pack pinched her shoulders. She shrugged but didn't complain. She was on a mission.

They turned a corner, and Virg waved from his truck. He pulled onto the road and honked. Stevie and Tucker jumped in the bed. Josh helped Emma, then climbed in beside her.

"Do we have everyone?" Dr. Woolf did a head count, then pounded on the truck cab. "Next stop, Cedar Hills Farm."

****

I jerked awake, swaying. Trees blurred in my vision, and I rubbed my eyes.

"You okay?" Brian held the reins around me, his warmth surrounding me.

An ache in my feet made me wince. "How long was I out this time?"

"Not that long, but you needed it. You're still recovering."

"Maybe." I frowned at him. "But now I need to walk, or I'll get frostbite in my toes."

He slid from the horse's back and dismounted, placing my feet on the ground and swaying. He grabbed my arm, and I pushed him away. A red blush rose to his cheeks. I had to push him away. Didn't he understand? The kiss changed everything. What a dork. Once again, he'd ruined everything.

I took a step, and my feet stung. I winced. A snowflake landed on my arm, and I glanced at him.

He nodded. "It's snowing again."

I glared at him.

He held his hands up. "I'm not making it snow. You can't blame this on me." He walked away leading Top Hat.

I gritted my teeth and jogged to catch up to him. "Sorry?" That was a lame apology. My stomach ached with hunger as snowflakes pelted my face.

Oscar sniffed scents at the side of the road.

Brian glanced at me. "We'd better find another place to shelter and warm up. We're soaked and…" His voice trailed off.

Hypothermia.

That's what he didn't say, but my toes weren't warming up. I couldn't feel them at all, and the snow fell in larger flakes, obscuring the dog the farther ahead he ran. I scanned through the trees searching for a roof, or a road, or signs of civilization. Trees lay in piles at the side of the road.

"At least the road is cleared here." I peered at Brian, but he ignored me. Did I really want his attention? I shivered, too miserable to care. I held up my wrist, 7:11.

Another elk called through the forest, forlorn and melancholy.

Chapter Fourteen

Snow pelted his face, and Brian squinted. He led Top Hat, and Olivia walked beside him, a hand on his shoulder. Was it for strength, or so she wouldn't wander off in the blinding snow and get lost? It wasn't for solace. He'd never be able to provide that. He plodded on. Oscar barked in the distance.

"Stupid dog," Olivia muttered.

Why was she always so negative? She had a chip on her shoulder, but why? She'd lost her whole family, but so had he. Her hand trembled on his shoulder, and he glanced over his shoulder. Were her lips blue? They needed to find a cabin, a place with a fireplace. There were lots of cabins up here, right? Maybe Oscar had found one.

He followed the dog's barks. A cabin came into view. Its roof sagged, but it had a chimney. "There." He pointed, and Olivia nodded, her teeth chattering.

She needed heat and food. He had to work fast, but what he wanted to do was hold her in his arms and warm her up. How, though, when he could hardly keep himself warm? They needed that cabin and a fire, quick. Olivia's teeth chattered, and she stumbled behind him as he approached the porch.

"Hold Top Hat, while I check it out."

She nodded like a zombie, and Top Hat shook his

head. She nuzzled into the horse's shoulder and put her hands under his mane. He sighed. This shelter better work or she'd freeze, and he wasn't going to let that happen.

He clomped up the steps and across the porch. A board cracked and broke. He jumped back and stepped around it. This place was falling apart. He pushed the door open, and the hinges squeaked. Oscar pushed past him and ran with his nose to the ground, sniffing as he explored every corner for a morsel to eat.

A fireplace stood against the wall opposite the door, but snow filtered down into the firebox. The floor had patches of ice in places. The roof leaked. Great. He scanned the room for firewood. It was outside under the snow if there was any. The walls and roof gave some protection from the wind and snow, though. At least that was something.

He picked his way across the rotten porch. "It's not the best, but it'll provide some shelter from the wind and snow."

"What about Top Hat?" She huddled against the horse who swung his head around to cradle her.

Brian shrugged. What could he say? How about the truth. "The porch is rotten, and the roof leaks. He can't come inside like at the lean-to."

She glared at him. "Top Hat can't stay outside in the snow." She ran her hands over the horse's face.

She was freezing, and all she worried about was the horse. She cared about that horse more than herself, and that was going to make her sick again if he didn't do something fast. Brian scanned the trees and brush around the cabin. "We could tie him to the branches of that tree, see?" He pointed. "There's no snow under it." Would she agree? She had to, but what if she didn't? He clenched his jaw.

She walked the horse under the tree branches. "I guess this will work until the snow stops." She tied the reins to a branch. "Is there wood for a fire, at least?"

"There must be." There had to be, right?

He tromped around the cabin and found a stack covered with snow. He rubbed his hands together to warm them before dismantling the pile and loading up his arms.

He rounded the corner. "Jackpot."

Oscar breezed past him. His doggy face was comical, but he didn't have the energy to laugh. She followed the dog into the cabin, her face gray and blank.

****

Smoke filled the cabin, and dust drifted in the air as Oscar continued to search for food. I held my stinging fingers to the fire. My teeth chattered. I held up the watch, 8:31. At least the sun had risen.

I sat, and my throat tightened. I coughed. "What's wrong? I'm gagging on smoke, and the fire's not even warm."

"The draft isn't pulling. The chimney must have collapsed inside toward the top." Brian scowled at the hearth.

"At least we're out of the wind." I rubbed my fingers together. The wind blew, and snow tapped the windows on one side of the house. "This is a whiteout. Dad talked about them, but I've never been in one." I held my arms around my torso. Claustrophobia much? "Let's hope it doesn't last much longer." I glanced at the watch.

"We're in the mountains. This storm could last for hours or days. We don't know. Want to share the time?"

"8:54. That's a.m., in case you were wondering." I sighed, my chest aching, but was it from smoke, grief, or illness? I couldn't afford to get sick again, not in the mountains in a blizzard.

****

She lay on the floor in front of the fire with Oscar curled up beside her. He laid on the other side of the dog. He couldn't sleep, but her regular breathing calmed him. She slept so much, but she wasn't vomiting, and she hadn't developed a fever. Mrs. Z was going to murder him. They'd missed the entire birthday party and the cake.

The wind whistled through the walls, and the fire smoked, but they were out of the storm. Light was fading already. He glanced at O laying on her side. Was she shivering? The fire didn't even heat the room. What a waste of good wood.

A thump came from the porch, and Brian stood without making a sound. Oscar jumped to his feet and growled and sniffed the base of the door.

O sat with a start. "What was that?"

The glow from the fireplace filled the room, and he wanted to switch it off like an electric light. Electricity. That would solve their heating problem, but this rickety old cabin didn't have wall heaters. It was rotting away and filled with smoke from the fire. The smoke would attract anyone out in the storm. The Brewsters?

He glanced at Olivia. Was it those asshole brothers? He moved toward the rustling on the other side of the front door. Something was on the porch.

"What's out there?" she whispered.

"Shhh." Brian stood and moved to a window. Oscar growled again as Brian peered into the snowy dark.

"What do you see?" She crouched low. "Is it Perry?"

"Shhh. I don't know." He scanned the room for a weapon and picked up the hatchet. She had the gun, but he wouldn't need that, would he? He'd protect her one way or another.

Oscar growled, and Brian grabbed for his collar, but the dog escaped his grasp.

"Look at him," Olivia croaked. "Is it a bear?"

His throat closed. Oscar the gangly puppy was gone, and in his place was a fierce guard dog. The hair stood on Oscar's back, and he growled again.

"Don't let him out," Brian whispered. "If it's a wild animal, he'll get torn to shreds." He pulled the curtain back an inch to expose the snow-filled landscape.

"Wait. If it's a bear, Top Hat would be going nuts." She rushed to one of the windows and peered out into the snow. Top Hat stood head up, ears perked toward something on the porch. "It must be a person." She put a hand to her throat. "Please not the Brewsters."

Oscar growled deep in his chest and rushed to Brian's side. He reached for the dog's collar again, but again he missed. The dog took his position by the front door and whined.

"Where's the gun?" he asked.

"What?" She rummaged through her bag and pulled out the revolver. "Mr. G only gave us five bullets." She held them out to him. "He didn't think we'd—"

Brian held up a finger and scanned the yard and the driveway.

Oscar barked. She grabbed his collar and pulled him to her, clamping her hands around his nose. He squirmed, but she sat on him. The dog grew quiet, his ears perked toward the snuffling by the door.

"Did you hear that?" She held the squirming dog. "Are they at the door?"

Brian tiptoed to the door. He tapped the door with the gun. A growl emanated from deep in Oscar's chest. A squeak and more shuffling came from the porch. He grabbed the knob and flung the door open. A striped tail waddled off the porch and into the snow.

He sighed and collapsed against the doorframe. "Not the Brewsters." He shut the door and leaned against it. Olivia released Oscar, who ran to the door whining. She lifted her wrist and caressed the watch face.

"What time is it? We should probably try to sleep a bit mo—"

"It's 9:14, and I'm not staying here another minute. I'm freezing, and it's smokey, and I don't feel safe." She took the gun from him and shoved it in the pack.

"But—"

"The snow has stopped, and if the Brewsters—" She stood and brushed dust from her pants.

"Wai—" He stared out the window into the darkness. He could make out Top Hat's black head against the snow. He stood ears pricked as he gazed at the house. He was thirsty and hungry. She was right. They had to leave and find water for the horse, and a cabin with a working fireplace.

She brushed past him and onto the porch without a glance at him. What did he expect? He sighed. Why did he ever kiss her, twice? He was a dork. He'd ruined any chance he had. He followed her out the door. She led Top Hat from under the tree and swung onto his back.

She reached a hand, and Brian swung up behind her. She needed his warmth, but what did he need? He had to wait for her to decide.

He put his arms around her, and she stiffened but didn't push him away. If only he could take the kisses back. Would that change this awkwardness between them?

He couldn't take those kisses back, but he didn't want to.

****

The road shone like ice. I held Top Hat's reins, and he walked between me and Brian. I could pretend I was alone, and my brain could process thought a little better than when he was right beside me. I needed space to think.

If I had my phone, I'd take a photo of the trees so tall and the mountains we could see in the gaps, but those days were over. Besides, this scene was beautiful but deadly, and it would remind me of my time up here with Brian, and did I really want that?

A tunnel created by the trees left standing channeled a brisk wind that blew snow into my eyes. Top Hat put his head down, huge puffs of steam filling the air with every breath. I glanced at Brian. What was this strange tingle in my belly?

A flake landed on my hand. I shivered. Would I ever be warm again? Was I making up an excuse to be close to him? It was uphill all the way, as Grandpa used to say, and it kept my blood flowing, heating my core but not enough to stop the shivering. Even Oscar had slowed down, like the cold stole his energy.

"Stupid Samson. Why did we agree to do this?" I patted Top Hat's cold neck. "Top Hat can't go much farther without hay and water." My teeth chattered as I glanced at Brian.

He frowned but wouldn't meet my eyes. He

tightened the strings on his hood and kept walking. I shivered. My jacket was waterproof, but not windproof. I hadn't needed windproof when I'd left the house for the barn.

The wind was relentless. I scanned the clouds for a bright spot that would be the sun. It was low in the sky, setting.

"If we don't get to Franklin soon, we'll die from hypothermia." Brian blew on his fingers.

I tucked my hands under my armpits, but my nose and cheekbones ached with cold.

"We'll get there quicker if we ride." Top Hat groaned as I mounted and reached for Brian's hand. He swung up behind me as though we'd done it a thousand times, and I drank in his warmth like a sponge.

"You're freezing." He wrapped his arms around me.

I leaned into him, too cold to sort out the butterflies fluttering in my chest.

"Samson lied to us." Brian tightened his hold on me. "He would have said anything to get those meds for Gracie."

Top Hat flipped his nose up and pulled against the bit. He walked slower and swatted his tail. "I know. You want to go home. Me too." I nudged Top Hat, and he walked faster. "Samson was desperate to save Gracie, but what about us? Did he know about the snowstorm?"

"I would have done the same if it would save my child." Brian's breath tickled the back of my neck as he spoke, and I shivered.

"Do you think we'll survive without electricity or medicine?" I shuddered. "Don't answer that. I don't really want an answer. At least some of us survived the novel hep A outbreak."

"This is exactly why history is so important. Novel hep A hit us like a pandemic, like the flu pandemic in 1918. A lot of people died of the flu, but a lot survived too. It wasn't the end of the world."

"Why is that important?"

Did he have to nerd out on me now? He shook his head, and I bristled.

"We know people have survived much worse than this. Sure, people died, but not everyone. We aren't used to living without roads, electricity, or running water. We've forgotten how to live in the way people did for thousands of years."

I frowned at him. "How do we relearn that now after we depended on electricity, phones, hospitals fully stocked with meds. We took it all for granted."

This conversation hurt my head. Images of Grandpa Billy in his sickbed haunted my thoughts. I rubbed my temples. "It seems like the Dark Ages all over again. If we could just get the meds, maybe that will help us until the new doctor arrives. That will save Gracie, and Mary's grandparents. But first we have to save ourselves."

Brian's body stiffened. "You don't think we'll survive this?" He glared at me. "We will. We'll get to Franklin and bring back the meds for Gracie and all of Cedarville because—"

"We have Top Hat?" I ran my hand down the horse's warm neck. Brian the optimist. I glanced into the forest as a familiar sting started behind my eyes. It was too late for my family, but not Gracie. Not yet anyway, or Cedarville, but we had to hurry. If it weren't for this snowstorm—

I cleared my throat. "So, you want to be the hero,

don't you?"

"Not really, but—" Brian glanced at the sky. "Oh no."

A sting hit my face. "Really? We won't last long in sleet." I held my watch close to my face.

"Time?"

"9:38. Still morning."

"We need shelter, fast." Brian scanned the sides of the road. I did too for a driveway or signs of a cabin.

Chapter Fifteen

The world was white, and the wind blew right through my hoodie. Top Hat walked with short, stiff steps. He needed to keep moving as much as we did. He plowed through a foot of snow covering the 96. Light snowflakes drifted to the ground.

"The Brewsters are long gone, right?"

Brian sat behind me on Top Hat, his warmth ever present in my mind. He shrugged, about to reply, but Oscar burst from the underbrush and trotted by us. Top Hat tossed his head, and I flinched. I tightened the reins in my hands, preparing for him to bolt.

A branch snapped off a tree, and a blizzard of soft snow cascaded to the ground. An icy rush cascaded over his head and neck. Top Hat spooked, and Brian gripped my waist as I wobbled, grabbing the saddle horn for balance.

"It's okay, boy." Snow fell in an avalanche from another branch, and I tightened my hood.

He marched on, ears pricked forward at attention. Oscar grinned up at us with snow clinging to his shaggy face. I envied his thick fur that protected him from these frigid temperatures.

The snow began falling in large flakes, hushing the world, as we rode through the winter wonderland. This might be fun if we had a warm cabin to warm up in, if there was hot soup waiting for us, if there was a warm fire—

Why was I so tired? Was this hypothermia?

Brian pointed into the distance. The roof of a cabin came into view. It hunkered in the trees off 96 crushed under the weight of a massive Douglas fir.

"That one won't work." I glanced at him as his shoulders sagged. I tensed with a shiver. He couldn't give up. We'd both die if he gave up.

A crow cawed and swept through the clearing, a stark relief against the white backdrop. It landed on a branch and cawed a warning, just like—

It meant nothing. Superstitions had no place here with us. I glanced at Brian, and he cocked an eyebrow at me.

"We have to find shelter."

I nodded, placing a hand under Top Hat's mane, and he turned to touch my foot with his nose. I shivered as he plodded through a foot and a half of snow.

Another steep pitched cabin roof came into view, and Top Hat whinnied. Did he smell hay? Oscar bounded to a ridge. I gasped. "He's going to—"

Brian hopped off and went after him.

"That stupid dog is going to get us all killed." My shoulders relaxed as the dog turned and sniffed his way away from the ledge.

"Oscar isn't stupid." Brian shook his head at me and waded to the cabin, checking the windows and the door. "This cabin seems solid," he called. "I'll see if I can get inside."

"What about Top Hat?" Oscar circled back to sniff Top Hat's nose, and the horse snorted at him. Oscar raced away. I reined the horse to the back of the cabin, the shelter of a carport attached to the cabin beckoned. Was that a stall? Oscar ran ahead and sniffed at some shelves built on the cabin wall under the carport. Cars. This wouldn't be used for cars anymore. The conversion to a stall made a lot of sense.

"It's perfect. This cabin is going to save our lives. I hope there's food." I scanned the covered space, the smell of oil still hanging in the air from years of cars parked in the space.

Brian shuffled around the cabin and under the carport. A door with a couple of steps stood in the middle of the wall. Brian reached for the doorknob. "I'll check."

"I'll get Top Hat bedded down." I jumped from Top Hat's back, pain shooting up my legs. I winced. My feet were frozen solid.

"Are you okay?" Brian frowned and reached a hand toward me.

I waved him off. "I'm good."

"I'll get a fire started, then see if there's canned food. Come, Oscar."

The dog ran up to Brian who grabbed a rag by the back door. He rubbed down the dog, opened the door, and then they disappeared into the cabin.

A half wall ran across the back fashioned out of fence boards. "Oh, Top Hat, a stall and hay." I scratched his ears. "And a bucket for water? This place is a castle."

I led Top Hat into the stall and unsaddled him with aching fingers. I slipped the bridle off, taking care not to hit his teeth with the bit, then slipped a halter over his head. I checked the pail. It looked fresh and clean. He sniffed the bucket, then drank. How was it not frozen? Someone must have been here in the last day or two.

A pile of hay lay in a mound by the back wall. I

threw Top Hat an armful. He nickered and, grabbing a bite, shook it until a mouthful separated from the pile. He stood munching with his eyes closed, and I checked the shelves on the wall. A brush and a hoof pick, jackpot.

"You're such a good boy." Top Hat sighed and chewed as I brushed the crusty sweat from him, warming up in the process. "You deserve a rub down." I leaned into his shoulder. "I will never let Perry or Aaron take you. You know that, right?"

Snow fell in whispers on the roof and trees, the flakes large and wet. It was mesmerizing, peaceful. I pressed my nose into the soft fur under his mane. Tears sprang to my eyes, and I let them fall.

"Thank you, Top Hat," I mumbled into his neck. He turned his head as if embracing me, his jaws munching hay. "You rest now. Who knows how long we'll stay here."

I let myself out of the stall, lifted my pack, and threw it over my shoulder. A sharp crack shot through the forest. I ducked. Gunfire? I waited for another shot, but it never came. Top Hat snorted and pushed his nose into the hay, pulling out another bite.

I sighed and let myself in the back door. Brian sat on the couch in front of the fireplace, the wood crackling and hissing, the clean wood perfuming the air.

My stomach rumbled as I shuffled into the living room. I twisted the watch on my wrist. Grandpa.

The weight of the watch calmed me. I wiped the crystal face clean with my thumb. 10:18. It had been a long year today, already. A fire crackled in the fireplace, and a cooking grate held a pot above the flames. I sat on the hearth, setting my pack on the floor by an overstuffed chair.

"What was that bang?" Brian glanced at me from the fire. "Sounded like a gun?"

"Must have been a branch snapping off a tree. It's not the Brewsters, or they'd be trying to get inside by now." I clenched my jaw to stop my teeth from chattering. "Made me jump, though."

"Me too. Oscar jumped a foot but didn't bark." He patted the dog's back. "On a survival note, I found their food supply: flour, sugar, salt, pepper. No fruit or veggies, but I didn't expect that. There's some canned stuff and an unopened box of saltines. They aren't too stale." He bit a cracker in half, spewing crumbs down his front. "I put some on the table."

Another crash sounded outside, and I put a hand to my throat. Brian rose and pulled back the curtains. Snow was raining down the side of a tree along the driveway.

"Same crack, so definitely a branch." Brian dropped the curtain and returned to stir the pot on the grate.

"I could eat a—"

Brian tilted his head and frowned. "Say sorry, Top Hat."

My stomach growled again, but I had other concerns right now.

"I found an outhouse out the front door to right of the porch." He stirred the pot, then put the lid back on.

Heat rose to my cheeks, but now wasn't the time to be shy. "That was my next question." I scanned the shelves lined with books on my way out the door. Whose cabin was this?

"Follow my footprints. It's pretty nice for an outhouse. Still smells like cedar."

I shook my head. "I can't believe we found this place. Oscar?"

The dog thumped his tail on the floor but didn't offer to follow me. "Fine. Let me get eaten by wild animals."

Brian shrugged as I zipped my jacket. I followed his footsteps through the dark. The wind had grown stronger, and the snow was blowing sideways. I turned. The cabin glowed, golden light pouring from every window and smoke rising from the chimney. I opened the door to the outhouse, and the tang of fresh cut cedar filled the air. I scanned for spiders. Did we even bring a flashlight? I sighed. At least I didn't have to go behind a tree.

****

I rushed back to the small cabin, warm air enveloping me as I closed the door. I shrugged out of my hoodie and scanned the room as the fire snapped. I wanted to sink into the couch. I would put my feet up on the coffee table in front of the fire...

Brian's pack covered the cushions, though. A chair sat angled to catch the warmth from the fire. Oscar lay sprawled under a coffee table, so it must be the perfect spot. In a corner to the left of the fireplace, a table and chairs were set up, windows surrounding the quaint scene. I shivered. The heat from the fire hadn't reached into the corners yet. I needed to make up my mind and sit down already.

This cabin had everything, a kitchen with cabinets and a metal sink set in a wooden countertop in the corner opposite the table. It would be warm and cozy soon. The back door stood opposite the front.

"Grandpa Billy would have called it a shotgun house." My chest tightened from missing him.

"A what?" Brian knelt by the fire, arranging a pot on a grate over the flames.

"Because you could shoot a bullet through the front, and it would exit out the back without hitting a wall or window, or a person." I shrugged out of my backpack, the weight of the gun clunking on the wood floor. My stomach rumbled, and my head spun.

Was I getting sick again? I gazed at the wall of books that lined the back wall of the living room, and a hall ran on the other side of the wall, creating a hallway to bedrooms, maybe? My stomach flipped. Brian had kissed me.

Brian lifted the lid of the pot, the aroma of chili filling the room. I'd eat anything at this point. My mouth watered as he stirred. He acted like he did this every day. I shook my head. I had to clear my head. I perched on the arm of an overstuffed chair by fire, warmth enveloping me. The bedrooms would be freezing. Would we use the bedrooms? Would we sleep—

Not together. We had a warm fireplace here.

I needed a diversion from my own thoughts. I glanced around the cabin. There were more windows than walls. The owners must love the mountain views from this little oasis. Brian walked to a window and watched the falling snow that blocked our view. My stomach rumbled again.

I stood. "A hungry stomach has no ears, or so Grandpa Billy used to say."

Brian crossed the room to the kitchen. "Fontaine?"

"Yep. I figured you get that one." I walked to the table and shoved a cracker in my mouth, crumbs tumbling to the floor.

He seemed so calm. Was he as awkward as I was about our situation?

"Wait until you see this." He pulled back a curtain

to reveal shelves lined with cans of chili, tuna, and assorted soups. "And this." He held up a kerosene lantern.

"Food and light?" I swayed and gripped the table.

"Are you okay?" Brian rushed to my side. "You need to sit down. You're white as a sheet." He pulled out the wooden chair closest to the fire.

"You must be starving."

"The food smells so good." I held my stomach. "Is it ready?"

"It's warm at least. I'll dish us up." He carried two bowls to the hearth and spooned chili into them.

The ripple of muscles in his arms mesmerized me, again. Where did he get muscles? Another wave of dizziness hit, and I leaned my head in my hands with my elbows on the table. I followed Brian's movements from under my lashes. Was he getting—less dorky? I must be sick.

The fire snapped, and the cabin walls creaked as they expanded with the warmth. The mantel clock chimed the half hour. That meant someone had been here in the last week. Where did they go? What would we do if they came back, and we were here eating their chili? I did have the gun. The fire cracked, and I jumped.

Oscar rolled over in front of the fireplace, one eye on Brian and the food he dished into bowls. Brian put the lid back on the pot, oblivious to the dog's attentions.

"Oscar already ate, so don't give him more." He patted Oscar's side. "He had chili for dinner too, didn't you." Oscar's tail thumped the floor. Brian stood and brought the full bowls to the table.

"This cabin has everything. Why couldn't we have found it first?" I glanced at Brian.

He nodded, placing a bowl in front of me, then grabbing a spoon. "It's perfect. We can rest here tonight and leave in the morning if the snow stops by then."

I spooned chili into my mouth and chewed slowly, savoring the spicy beans as snow swirled past the windows. We needed shelter and rest, but we couldn't stay long. A shudder wracked my body. Would I be ready?

Chapter Sixteen

Emma planted her feet, her hands on her hips. The tiny bedroom radiated light with yellow paint and an elephant lamp on a chest of drawers. The child in the bed lay motionless as she took her pulse.

Samson hovered by the bed, staring at the floor. Gracie meant more to him than life itself, but he sent Olivia and Brian into a mountain storm for what? A potion?

Dr. Johnson pulled the stethoscope from his ears and walked into the hallway. "She isn't improving, but she's no worse, so the milk thistle could still help her liver if we can get it to her in the next day or two." He glanced at Samson and cleared his throat. "So, when did you send Brian and Olivia—"

Barb grabbed Samson's arm. "What did you do?"

He stared at the floor, shaking his head.

"We got a transmission from Franklin. They are snowed in again, and the storm is still raging." She stabbed a finger at his chest. "Tell me you didn't send those sweet kids into that snowstorm."

Dr. Johnson pulled his glasses off and glanced from Samson to Barb. Emma's chest hurt watching the scene play out. A father doing what he had to for his beloved child at the expense of others. Samson crossed his arms. Gracie lay, a fragile leaf rustling under the covers of her bed.

"It's Gracie, hon." Samson glanced at his wife.

"Oh no, Samson." Barb put her face in her hands.

Emma placed a hand on Barb's shoulder. She jumped away, then collapsed into Emma's arm. Barb's anger and Samson's anguish were horrifying to witness. Dr. Johnson cleared his throat and waited for Barb to stop crying.

"If it's any consolation, we all need another doctor. If those two young people bring her back along with more of the medicines, they'll be heroes." Dr. Johnson perused a file that held Gracie's chart.

"Thank you, Doctor. I didn't mean for anything bad to hap—"

"Samson, honey, you could have gone yourself." Barb clasped her hands as if in prayer. Samson uncrossed his arms and clenched his fists. His biceps rippled under his flannel shirt.

Dr. Johnson took a step back and cocked an eyebrow at Emma. She sighed. Gracie whined, and Samson grimaced.

"See?" He pointed a finger at his daughter's tiny body as she shook with fever.

Barb rushed to Gracie and held her hand. "Mommy's here. Shhh, darling."

Emma took a step forward. Could she say what she'd planned? Samson's act of selfishness could cost two of her friends their lives. She had to say something, or she'd explode.

"Mr. and Mrs. Coffey, you must understand that it's been getting colder since they left, which means it's snowing in the mountains." She glared at Samson, who gazed at his daughter.

"I know, but—"

"But nothing." Dr. Woolf stepped into the room, preparing for battle. "You sent them into danger. We all need the new doctor, but you knew about the storm warning, that hypothermia—"

Dr. Johnson held up a hand to stop Dr. Woolf, then turned to Samson. "You did what you felt you had to. Now let's hope they make it there and back. It could save Gracie and so many others." He glanced over his bifocals at Emma.

Samson hung his head. Barb took her husband's hand, tears wetting her cheeks. "You told them it would only take a couple hours, didn't you." Her shoulders shook, and she sobbed. "You did it for Gracie."

He rubbed his forehead and stared at his boots. "I'm losing my mind here. I can't let Gracie die. What was I supposed to do?"

"You could have gone yourself." Barb's matter-of-fact voice startled Emma.

"Mommy," Gracie called again, her breath raspy and hoarse.

"The fence, the cows, the milk, the hay, the illness, it's too much—" he mumbled.

"I'm going to tent her with a steam pot, for now. We'll just have to hope Olivia and Brian make it back with the doctor." Dr. Johnson dropped the clipboard to his side. "Emma?"

"I'm on it."

Dr. Johnson walked out of the room, and Emma followed. She resisted the temptation to look over her shoulder. Samson's eyes haunted her. He'd proven he would do anything for Gracie, for his family, but to send Olivia and Brian to Franklin? She clenched her jaw. He'd better hope nothing happened to them, or he'd regret it, Gracie or no Gracie. She rolled her shoulders and followed Dr. Johnson to the kitchen fire. She filled a teapot with hot water. Doing something, anything, was better than this waiting game.

She gazed out the window. Mount Rainier stood in the distance behind the clouds. Olivia and Brian were up there, but were they okay?

****

I rubbed my eyes and scanned the room, warm with the glow of a fire.

Where was I?

The bookcase on the back wall came into focus. They were all hardback books. I hadn't noticed that before. I glanced at the vaulted ceiling.

Oh, right. It was Sunday, and we were on our way to Franklin.

I stretched. My legs ached from too many hours in the saddle. I groaned as the fire crackled in the fireplace, and glanced at Grandpa Billy's watch. 10:26. It was our second day in the mountains, and I was on my umpteenth nap already. Why was I so groggy?

Brian smiled at me. "Nice sleep?"

I cocked my eyebrow at him. "Smart-ass." The tang of smoke filled the air. I glanced at the trees outside the window, their branches fat with snow.

"The snow stopped, so we can leave." He stood and brushed his hands on the seat of his pants.

"Leave?" I jumped to my feet. "How long was I out? How deep is the snow? Where's Oscar? Is Top—"

Brian held his hands up. "Whoa. Everyone is fine. The storm is over, and we can leave."

He waited as I let that sink into my tired brain. I

walked to a window and lifted the curtain to the winter wonderland. Patches of blue peeked through the clouds. Was something going right for a change?

The fire crackled in the hearth, and a loud rip came from the vicinity of the fire. A stench filled the air.

"What was th—" I put a hand over my nose and mouth and waved the air in front of my face. "Aww."

"What?" Brian sniffed the air.

I scrunched my nose. "It was you." I backed away from him, and Oscar thumped his tail on the floor.

"Whoa, Nellie." He held his nose. "That was not me." He fanned the air with a dish towel. "Oscar."

Oscar rolled on his back and assaulted us with another blast.

"Don't excite him." I held my hand over my nose, as he released yet another blast. "Oh man, let him outside." My words twanged as I held my nose. I slipped on my boots and shrugged into my jacket. "I'll take him out. I have to saddle Top Hat anyway. Maybe Oscar will, you know, out in the yard."

Brian gripped the counter, laughing so hard he couldn't stand. "It must have been the chili."

Oscar squirmed with delight, crop-dusting the living room. Grandpa Billy would have had a field day with this farting dog.

Brian shook a finger at him. "You old farter. No more chili for you."

I opened the door. Oscar ran out, and I followed him, holding my nose. A gust blew snow against my face and cleared the putrid stench from my nostrils. He was a gas factory.

Oscar ran into the snow and disappeared around the corner of the cabin, then reappeared racing to me and sliding into my legs.

Oh no. Zoomies.

He jumped and woofed in my face, ran back into the snow, an expression of sheer happiness on his doggie face. I screamed and laughed as he barreled through the drifts, his hair flying, breaking wind as he ran. He plowed his nose through the deep snow and rolled, digging his way to the carport.

Brian's deep laughter boomed from inside the cabin. He stood in a window and shrugged into his jacket, his arm muscles rippling. I turned away, heat rushing into my cheeks. Don't make it weird.

I needed Brian more than ever. He was good at this survivor stuff, making fires and cooking dinner. I shivered. I'd been ignoring him for eight years, so I could do that a bit longer, right?

I scanned the yard, my breath creating clouds of vapor. The snow muffled my footsteps and brightened the world. Smoke spiraled from the chimney into the sky. Top Hat nickered. I opened the stall and ran my hands over his back and neck. He was dry, and his winter coat was thick and warm.

"Let me tell you something, horse, we can't keep stopping every couple of hours for a little snow. We have to get to Franklin." I sighed. Who was I kidding. "Do you think we can do this?"

I pushed my nose into Top Hat's neck. He wrapped his head around me in his warmth as if to say, "Yes. We are going to do this."

I reached for the saddle as a gust of wind blew snow under the carport.

No. I stared into the yard as Oscar trotted through the deep drifts. Snow fell in a blur of white. Another storm so soon? Would we ever get a break? I let my arms drop to my sides.

Oscar ran into the shelter and shook his fur, and Top Hat snorted and took a mouthful of hay. He scratched at the door, and Brian opened it. Our eyes met, and he shrugged.

"Looks like we're stuck here."

****

A thick fog surrounded the cabin, and snowflakes swirled in the mist. The wind blew snow into graceful drifts. Would the storm never end? Brian scratched out notes on a sheet of paper. He hadn't uttered a complaint, a word of wisdom, a worry, nothing—I glanced at my watch—in the last hour. He might have said "at least we have shelter," but he sat writing in silence.

The fire crackled in the fireplace, and the cream curtains on all the windows hung open to a white world. We'd be here until the fog lifted or the storm ended or both.

If I had my journal, I'd—

What? Capture our trek into danger? I'd never get excited about snow ever again. It was dangerous, but so was Brian. I couldn't relive that kiss one more time, but I was. It never stopped. A shiver passed over my body, even with the warmth from the fire. We had faced death together, and this cabin had saved us, but now snow trapped us here. I sighed. When would it end?

Grandpa Billy had a word for this, "Cabin fever." It made me listless. I napped and paced, but Brian brooded, and frowned, and replied in monosyllabic grunts. I didn't recognize this angry silence from him, and the quiet left my skin crawling. He hunched over that piece of paper writing until I wanted to scream.

He pushed himself from the table, and I jerked to attention. Was this it? He held up the sheet of writing. "Want to hear my masterpiece?"

"What?" Masterpiece? Was the Dorkmeister back? I cocked an eyebrow. That would be better than moody-Brian. I sighed and nodded, and he cleared his throat.

I once knew a young man of wisdom,
who got trapped in a cabin by a snowstorm.
He woke up one day,
and cried out in dismay,
I'm stuck in the cabin of boredom.

I shook my head. "Masterpiece? The only thing you got right was cabin of boredom." I put my hand over my mouth to stop the laughter. "All this time, I thought you were planning our departure, and you've been writing limericks?"

"Is it that bad?" Brian frowned at me, his arms crossed.

The tension eased from my shoulders. Was he back? "Yes. It stinks as bad as one of Oscar's farts." I swatted the air, but he didn't look up or chuckle. He stared at his feet.

Cabin fever.

"We can't just sit here." He jumped to his feet.

I tensed. "We have to do just that, or we'll die."

He glared out the window. I had to think of something, or he was going to rush out into the snow.

He paced in front of the fireplace. "I don't care if it's still snowing. We have to leave."

"But there's at least two feet of snow out there."

"We must be close to Franklin. What time is it?"

I checked the watch. "Noon. We should eat lunch."

"If it's noon, there are hours of daylight. Come on,

we can make it." He glared at me.

I glared back, but his steely gaze wore me down. "But in a storm?"

He paced, like a caged animal. "We can't wait until the snow stops. Think of Gracie."

I stood and joined him by the window. Our roles were shifting, but I had no idea how to be the optimist, the cheerful one. The fog had risen, revealing the forest, yet snowflakes still fell in lazy spirals. I watched, mesmerized for a moment.

Under different circumstances this might have been romantic.

Don't go there.

Brian scoffed. Had he read my mind? Heat rose to my cheeks, and I shook my head.

He glared out the window. "Look. The snow's not as heavy. We can blaze a trail through that snow."

"No." I cringed, afraid of the cold, the wind, but staying seemed too much like defeat, and his frown was starting to worry me. Where was the Dorkmeister when I needed him?

"It's April, for God's sake. Why did freezing temps drop down to this elevation today of all days?" He plopped in a chair.

His silence grated on me. I shook my head. "Okay, after lunch."

"Really?" He glared at me.

What was the plan? To stay positive and give him a goal.

"We have one mission, remember?" I stood, my hands on my hips.

"Don't remind me." He hadn't raised his voice, but his harsh tone cut deep. "We leave in an hour."

I stepped back. Why was he being so impossible. He couldn't have it both ways, wanting to leave but not knowing how. He was right, though. The snow had kept us rushing from shelter to shelter between storms, and we almost froze. We needed a plan, or we'd—

Hypothermia.

I shrugged my shoulders and sighed.

"I didn't mean to sound so harsh." He bowed his head. "This isn't your fault."

"Maybe there are snowshoes in the cabin? They have everything else." I scanned the beams of the cabin. Were there snowshoes? Let there be snowshoes.

Brian nodded, scratching his chin. "Right. We could leave Top Hat here. It would be faster."

"That idea doesn't suck." I cocked an eyebrow at him. Had snowshoes hooked him?

Brian checked the ceiling. "Maybe they store stuff in the rafters. You check the carport. What we need is a snowplow."

"On it." I grabbed my coat and headed for the door, glancing over my shoulder.

Brian pulled a ladder from beside the fridge and climbed to the loft area over the bedrooms in the back of the cabin. I stopped at the back door as Brian's legs then feet disappeared into the attic space. He seemed distracted from his cabin fever episode. I'd missed his usual positive attitude, that was for sure.

Top Hat nickered as I stepped outside. The carport was dry, and the smell of horse manure mingled with car oil as I walked to the stall. Top Hat reached his head over the gate and touched noses with Oscar.

I rubbed my forehead. "Have you seen any snowshoes?"

Top Hat shook his head and stared at the cabin wall. I peered over my shoulder. Two sets of snowshoes hung on a nail high on the wall. "Did you know they were there this whole time?" I closed my eyes and hugged Top Hat. With snowshoes, not even the Brewster brothers could stop us.

Chapter Seventeen

The door creaked open, and Brian stepped out. His shoulders sagged, and he rubbed his eyes. I held my face in a blank look so I didn't ruin my surprise.

"No snowshoes." He sighed.

I pointed at the wall to the left of the door. He glanced up and shook his head.

"Seriously? This cabin is saving our lives again. I'll grab the pack." He disappeared into the house, a gentle smile of relief on his face.

I chuckled. "That means your vacation is over, boy." I patted his neck. "I better clean your stall and feed you quick."

I slipped a halter on Top Hat and snapped a long line to his halter. I led him through the deep snow out into the yard and tied the rope to a small tree.

"No funny business while I'm cleaning your stall, okay?" I patted his neck, then headed back to the stall, keeping him in my vision. The horse walked out into the middle of the yard and started pawing at the deep snow. Of course, he wanted to play. He'd been stuck in that stall for hours. He stuck his face into the snow until only his eyeballs showed, then he snorted. A plume of white billowed up. He jumped sideways with a squeal and a buck.

I gasped. "No, no, no." I struggled against the deep

snow to grab the lead rope before Top Hat broke it. Brian burst from the cabin.

"What's going on?" He stood under the carport as Oscar barked and ran zoomies around Top Hat, flowing through the snow, gliding over the surface as he leaped. Top Hat squealed and bucked, chasing after the dog. I reached for the rope as it pulled taut and snapped from the tree, sending a spray of snow into the air. It all happened in slow motion.

Oscar raced down the driveway, Top Hat bucking and snorting after him. I plowed after them for several steps but stopped, gasping for air. Horse and dog had disappeared. Brian raced after them in his canvas tennis shoes, slipping and sliding.

"Oscar. Top Hat." I hopped in Top Hat's tracks and caught up to Brian, but they were gone.

"They'll come back, right?" Brian frowned, lines creasing his forehead.

"Oscar might, but Top Hat could run back to Mr. G's." A shiver ran through me. We needed both animals for our survival. I held my head in my hands.

Brian grabbed my shoulder, and I followed the line of his pointing finger. Oscar and Top Hat were charging back down the drive straight toward us. I dove left, and Brian dove right. The underbrush rustled, and he yelled, his voice growing faint as Oscar ran past, the horse right behind.

I rushed to where Brian had fallen in the bushes but stopped waving my arms in the air to stop myself from falling. The sheer drop-off hidden by the undergrowth took my breath away. Long skid marks led to where Brian had disappeared over the edge. The pain in my chest hit me like the stab of a knife. Was he alive?

I filled my lungs with air and shouted. "Brian."

Nothing. *Oh my God.*

"Brian." I pulled off my hood, and snow stung my face with every flake. Where was he? I couldn't lose one more person I cared about. Wait. I cared about him?

Of course, I did, and I had to know if he was hurt. I couldn't lose him now, not now. My mind raced. What should I do?

Oscar returned and pressed past me to the cliff's edge. He barked.

"Stupid dog." I clenched my teeth. "This is your fault."

"Olivia?" His voice came to me muffled, as if he were a million miles away.

I pulled Oscar to me and hugged him. He was alive. *Thank all the goddesses.* "Brian." I scanned the drop but couldn't find him. He'd called me by my name, so this was serious. "Are you okay?"

"I landed on a ledge. My ankle hurts, but I'm fine." His voice rose from far below.

I clutched my hands, rubbing my numb fingers to warm them. He must be frozen by now. "Can you climb up?" I scanned the driveway for Top Hat. Where was he?

"No. It's a sheer wall of rock. There's nothing to hold on to."

I cringed as I scanned the expanse of the valley falling away from the ridge where I stood helpless. The enormity of the space filled my view, and I stepped back on wobbly legs. How would he ever climb up? The steep angle of the cliff hid him from view, but he was there somewhere. I reached out a hand. The wind picked up and whistled through my coat. Snow sprinkled down from the branches, and I shivered.

I had to do something. "Brian, I'm going to get a rope. I'll use Top Hat to pull you up, okay?"

"No. I'm too far down. You'll never find a rope long enough." His words fell flat against the snow, leaving a heavy silence hanging in the air.

I raced down the drive to the cabin, my smooth soled riding boots slipping and sliding. Rope. Rope. I couldn't lose Brian.

Oscar trotted up to Top Hat who sniffed the trees and bushes near the carport, looking for something to eat no doubt. "Look what you've done." I glared at them. They stood like two big dogs, oblivious to Brian's plight but aware that they'd misbehaved.

"Steady, boy." I put my hand on Top Hat's neck and took the frayed rope. He lifted his left hoof but stopped. "What's wrong?" I pulled on the lead, and he put his foot down but lurched. "Oh no. Really? What have you—"

I ran my hand down his leg. He flinched. Lame? No.

I stood and pulled on the rope. "Look, you did this, and now you have to help." The horse hobbled behind me to the carport. I threw the saddle on his back, cinching him tight, then pulled down two coils of rope and slung them over my shoulder. I clasped the lead rope with a shaking hand and led Top Hat to where Brian had disappeared. The horse limped the whole way.

I cupped my hands around my mouth and called, "I'm going to lower a rope." My frozen hands fumbled as I tied the two strands together. Hands be damned. I had to do this, even if it was on adrenaline.

"Brian."

No response. Where was he? Clouds cover hung low over the trees. I stared over the ledge. No Brian. I fastened the lead rope around the saddle horn and threw it over the edge.

"Stay." I glared at Top Hat, then Oscar. Oscar whined, but he sat.

Why didn't Brian answer? I grabbed the rope and sat on the edge of the cliff. The drop took my breath away, and Top Hat walked a couple steps away.

"Whoa." The rope slid through my frozen hands, burning them.

What was I doing? The wind blew stronger as I rolled onto my stomach. I clung to the rope. The smooth rock face provided nothing to brace myself on. Top Hat shifted again, and the rope slipped through my hands. If he decided to run now, I was screwed. I didn't have the strength to save Brian by myself. Damn it.

I kicked at the rock wall. Brian was right. The rope wasn't long enough, and my arms would give out before I ever reached him, anyway.

I glanced at the ledge. Brian's fall had compacted the snow, but his shoe prints led to a scramble of rocks in the opposite direction of the cabin. Beyond the ledge the drop was sheer for hundreds of feet. My stomach tightened. He was using the rough footholds and handholds to climb out. He could fall. What was he thinking? If he had any other choice, he would have taken it. What a mess.

"Brian?" I held my breath. "Brian?"

The tree boughs swayed in the wind. The fog had lifted, and the mountain became visible through a flurry of snow. The steep drop took my breath away.

"Brian." I called again.

I clung to the rope with my feet braced against the rock. The wind whistled through the trees, creating a ghostlike howl. Snow cascaded from above like mini avalanches. I glanced up as Oscar peered over the edge, wagging his tail. Did he think this was a game?

"Stay," I growled, and gripped the rope. I climbed the short distance, gasping for air. I pressed my foot against a rock, finding purchase with my leather-soled boot. I pulled myself up with shaky arms and eased my body over the top, gasping. Oscar barked, then whined, then crawled on his belly over the edge.

"Damn it, Oscar." I reached for his collar but missed. "No."

Oscar's claws scratched down the rock face, and he fell with a "yipe."

I stared at the empty spot. He barked from the ledge, his claws clicking on rock. Was he going after Brian?

"Good dog."

I pushed myself to a stand and leaned against Top Hat for warmth as the snow collected on my shoulders. I ran my thumb over Grandpa Billy's watch, the face smooth and cold. I tilted my wrist. 11:43.

Mount Rainier disappeared behind the clouds as the wind blew in a misty fog. I wiped my nose on the back of my hand. Was this our banquet of consequences? If it was, it sucked.

****

He clung to the rock cliff, his fingers stiff from the cold. *Don't look down.* He stared at a crack in the rock face and followed it to the right. How could he stop Olivia from endangering herself to save him? His heart constricted. He couldn't stop her from getting a rope, but if she fell…

He glanced to the right. If he could make it to the rock jumble, he might be okay, if it wasn't loose rock. He had to get out before she…

"Brian. Brian."

He clung to the ledge. How did he let her know he was okay when there didn't seem a way off this ledge?

"Brian. Where are you?" Her voice echoed over the valley.

He scanned the drop, clinging to the rock. What could he say to calm her when he couldn't calm himself?

"I'm on a ledge." He cringed at the expanse of the fall. *I'm so screwed.* The enormity of the space gave him vertigo. The steep angle of the cliff hid her from view, but she was there somewhere, and her concern gave him hope. The wind picked up and whistled through his shirt. How did he forget a coat? Snow sprinkled down from the branches, and he shivered.

"I'm going to get a rope."

"Don't. It's too dangerous. I'll find a way out." His words fell flat against the cliff, and the silence meant she was gone. He had to find a way off this ledge before she returned. He hobbled along the edge, his ankle unable to carry weight.

I'm so screwed.

Chapter Eighteen

I stared over the ledge, my toes tingling and numb. Top Hat filled the crisp air with vapor with each breath he took. Where were they? Were they climbing out or clinging to a rocky ledge somewhere? The hair rose on the back of my neck. How would they ever get out? I scanned the expansive valley. It was at least a thousand feet to the bottom, but Brian had only fallen twenty or so, right? Mount Rainier sat to the left at the end of the valley, majestic and serene.

I clenched my fists. Stupid Oscar. Why did he have to chase Top Hat?

Brian would have better luck if he hiked toward the highway where the slope wasn't so steep, but that would take hours. Maybe he has rock-climbing skills I didn't know about. Wasn't he an Eagle Scout?

Yeah, right. He was still screwed.

I sighed. "Top Hat, they're gone."

He nudged me, and I lifted my hand to his warm cheek. Snow began to fall, and the wind whistled through the valley. My stomach balled into a knot. A viselike grip tightened around my chest.

"Come on. There's nothing we can do here." I stomped my feet to get the blood flowing, then led Top Hat to the cabin. I glanced at the watch. 11:51 a.m. Had time slowed down? We'd lost our window of good weather. Franklin might as well be on the moon at this rate.

****

Top Hat limped behind me to the carport and into his stall. I unsaddled him, and I tossed him an armful of hay, then stumbled into the house. *What do I do now?* I paced before the windows clouded with condensation, and stared out at the snowflakes, "each one unique," as Brian would say. Was he a dork, or was he just smart, and where was he now?

I stirred the ashes in the fireplace and threw on some kindling. It caught, and I placed a larger piece on the flames. The least I could do was keep it warm in here. I sat on my knees in front of the warm fire and glanced around the cabin. Brian's kiss was a memory now. Would I ever get another one?

What? Was that his jacket?

It hung off the back of a chair. I stood and paced the room, images from my nightmares swirling through my brain. He heard me cry out and ran outside, didn't even stop to grab a coat. Crazy Dorkmeister.

My stomach fluttered. He cared, and I was just standing here. I scanned the overstuffed chairs, the plaid curtains, the fire crackling. What did I do now? I pressed my eyelids closed. Emma would call on the goddesses like her friends Lilli and Jade had. They'd survived the aftermath of the first storms, but I could tell she wasn't kidding. The goddesses seemed to listen to her. Maybe they'd listen to me?

"Please, all you beautiful goddesses, help him. Let him be okay."

My eyes burned from holding back tears, and a pain beat behind my breastbone. The snow would stop soon, right?

What did Emma say at the end of her appeal? Ah, yes.

So, mote it be.

****

I couldn't sit in the cabin waiting for one more minute. I shrugged into my jacket and tromped out the back door. Top Hat popped his head up as I stepped down the steps to the stall. I threw him more hay, and the clouds parted like magic.

Sunrays glinted off the glaciers on Mount Rainier. Now the sun shone. The mountain resembled a giant scoop of vanilla ice cream. It rose over 14,000 feet at the end of the valley. Brian was out there somewhere, right?

I grabbed the saddle and lifted the handle on the stall gate. I couldn't sit here doing nothing for one more minute. I had to find Brian before the Brewsters did, or before they returned.

The snow had dropped from all the branches, and everything dripped like a heavy rain. What did I expect. It was April, and the temperature had risen. The snow on the driveway on the porch sloshed with every step.

Damn those Brewsters. This was all their fault. I grabbed a brush and attacked Top Hat's back. He grunted and turned his giant head to nudge me.

"I know, you have a sore leg, but what about Brian?" I smoothed his hair with my hand.

A twig snapped on the driveway, and I scanned the area. Was it a deer? I glared down the driveway trying to track the sound. Oh no.

The Brewster brothers were back. I rushed from the stall, latched the gate, and rushed inside the cabin. I pulled the gun from my pack slipping into my jacket pocket. I inhaled and released the breath in a steady hiss, then opened the door. I stood on the porch as the Brewsters stepped out of the brush and onto the driveway.

Aaron held the rifle, but what was Perry holding? It looked like a long stick. I gasped. A bow?

Brian. Where are you?

He wasn't here, and I had to protect Top Hat. I stared at Aaron's tangled hair and Perry's unzipped jacket. There were holes in their drenched jeans. Wild boys sloshing through the melting snow in the mountains. This was insane. I glared at them. How would I use the gun if my hands weren't steady?

Perry's coat hem hung in tatters where Oscar had ripped it. They seemed smaller to me, drenched, dirty, and lost. Why had I been so afraid? Because they were unpredictable.

Perry notched an arrow and shot at the cabin. The arrow thunked into the snow five feet in front of the porch, then tipped into the melting snow. Laughter bubbled from the back of my throat. Was that supposed to frighten me?

"Give us the horse," Perry yelled.

"No." I clenched my teeth and tightened my grip on the gun.

"We'll see about that." Aaron raised the rifle and aimed at the horse.

"Stop." I took a step forward. Top Hat stood exposed under the open lean-to. I lifted the revolver with shaking hands.

Were they bluffing? I pointed it at Aaron. Perry grabbed Aaron's arm, and he swung the rifle toward his brother. A sharp report echoed off the valley walls.

Perry crumpled into the snow.

I gasped. "Perry." I pointed the gun at Aaron.

He fell to his knees in the slosh of melting snow. "Perry. Oh my God. Perry." He ran his fingers across Perry's forehead, brushing hair from his eyes.

I lowered my arms, and the shaking began, first in my lips, then in my hands. I couldn't speak, but I wanted to scream.

Aaron crouched over Perry's body. He blubbered something I couldn't understand, but Perry didn't move no matter how much Aaron shook him. I could see the snow turning a bright scarlet.

Brian was lost in the wilderness, and I had to do this, whatever this was.

I walked toward Perry, blood pounding in my ears, holding the gun.

Aaron jumped at sight of the gun and kicked the rifle in the bushes.

"Don't shoot. I didn't mean it."

Was that all he could think of to say?

He stood and grabbed a fistful of his hair in each hand. He sobbed. "Perry." Then he turned and, with arms pumping at his sides, sprinted down the driveway, leaving Perry in the wet snow.

"Perry." I slipped and skidded to his side, the shot still ringing in my ears. Was he dead?

Chapter Nineteen

A cloud obscured the sun, and the temperature dropped several degrees. I knelt beside Perry. I couldn't pull my gaze away from his pasty complexion. I wanted to run away, but if I left him here, he'd freeze. I glanced back at the cabin. How would I ever get to get him to the cabin by myself?

He lay drenched and sprawled on the ground. Hypothermia would kill him before the bullet in his leg did. I knelt beside his body. "You are not going to die. Not on my watch."

Was he already dead? He looked dead.

I bit my cheek. His pale skin had the same waxy sheen as Grandpa Billy's. He couldn't die. I shook my head to clear it. What would Emma do in this situation? She'd check for a pulse. Right. I reached out a shaky hand and put a finger on the carotid artery in his neck.

He had a heartbeat. I glanced at my watch. 12:21. It was still morning.

"Perry? We have to get you off the ground and into the cabin. Can you hear me? You need to warm up by the fire." He didn't respond. Did he hear a word I said?

I scanned the underbrush where Aaron had thrown the rifle. He was still out there.

I rushed to the carport and grabbed a canvas tarp from one of the shelves. If I could slide him onto the tarp,

I could pull him to the cabin. Why was I doing this? Perry broke up with me, right? And Brian kissed me, but he was lost, and now Perry's—

What? What was Perry? He was alive and needed help, and that's what I had to do now, help. I could feel my pulse pounding in my veins as I slipped and slid back to Perry.

Why didn't he wake up? I jostled his shoulder. "Perry. Perry."

He moaned.

"Don't you die, Perry Brewster."

How could I still care about him? Was that why I was doing this? I stared at Perry lying in the slush. Did I care? Of course, but not as a boyfriend, as a human being.

I spread the tarp on the ground beside Perry, then raised his head and shoulders and lifted his limp body onto it, then I did the same with his feet. Perry grunted with pain.

"I'm not dying." He opened his eyes and pushed my hands away. "What's the tarp for? Where's Aaron?"

"He ran away. So brave." I grabbed a corner of the tarp.

He placed a hand on his leg and winced. "He shot me?"

"To be fair, it was an accident." I knelt on the tarp. "I was going to roll you onto the tarp and pull you to the—"

"That's a stupid idea. You couldn't budge me." He grunted as he sat. "Give me a moment."

"Well what's your plan? Can you even walk?"

"I can try." He glared at me.

"Take your time, but you can't stay on this cold

ground." What was he thinking? What was I thinking? I couldn't pull him by myself, but could he stand, let alone walk?

"Give me your hand."

I reached out to him, and he clasped my hand. His was cold, and I slipped to a knee as he pulled. "Wait." I dug my boots into the slush and tugged with all my strength. He rose to his feet, and I grunted with the effort.

He draped his arm over my shoulder, and he hobbled. I bent under his weight, but somehow, we made it to the carport. Top Hat snorted.

"Easy boy," I called in a soothing voice between gasps for air. Perry weighed a ton for a skinny guy, and I lowered him onto a step as my stomach lurched. I'd pushed myself too hard. I groaned and rushed to the edge of the trees and vomited.

What was wrong with me? He didn't weigh that much.

My head pounded as I staggered back to the carport. Top Hat kept his eye on Perry. We'd made it this far, but how was I going to get his sorry ass into the cabin?

****

With every person I lost, I disappeared a little. I wiped my eyes and cradled my wet cheeks in my hands. Perry rested against the door. Had he fallen asleep? My stomach clenched. I had to wake him so he could walk. It was the only way to get him up the stairs and into the cabin. If he didn't, he'd die in this carport.

No. That wasn't going to happen. Steam from my breath surrounded me as I shook Perry's shoulder.

"Perry. Wake up." He didn't respond. I shook harder. "We have to get you into the cabin."

He groaned and opened one eye. "Olivia? Is this a—

"

I couldn't let him finish that thought. He was awake, and we had to move fast. "You made it this far. Now get up." I lifted his head and shoulders.

"Shit." He gritted his teeth. "Slow."

He tried to rise, and blood flowed from his leg wound. I took his hand and pulled as he grunted to a stand. We didn't have much time before I was going to collapse. He leaned on me, and I staggered, but we made it up the steps and hobbled together across the smooth wood floor to the couch.

I eased him onto the cushions, and he sighed before drifting into unconsciousness. How much blood had he lost? I added some wood to the fire, and it snapped and cracked, the smoke rising up the chimney and filling the cabin with the comforting smell of warmth and wood.

I shrugged out of my jacket and, grabbing a towel, wrapped his leg. Then I grabbed a blanket and tucked it around his torso, wet clothes and all. I'd never get his pants off him without hurting him.

I sat on the chair by the fireplace and pulled off my boots, then unlaced Perry's boots and put them by the door. I brought a glass of water to Perry, but he pushed it away.

Now what did I do? I'd exhausted all my first aid knowledge.

"Brian, where are you?" I willed him home as I opened the door and stepped outside in my stockinged feet.

I stood motionless. Was that movement? I stared down the driveway. Was it Aaron? A person trudged toward the cabin. Had the goddesses answered my prayer, or was it Aaron coming to finish what he'd started? A dog barked.

"Oscar?" I propelled myself out the door, my stockinged feet sinking in the snow. I ran. Oscar swung his limp tail and panted but didn't run to me or jump on me. "What happened to you too?" Brian's wet hair clung to his skull and dripped onto his snow-covered shoulders.

"You're back. How did you—You're back." I threw my arms around Brian, and we fell into the snow.

He coughed. "O." He clung to me as I helped him to his feet, and he pulled me to him and kissed my lips. I let him and held him to me as if all of life depended on our connection.

I sighed, and my tummy flipped as his gaze never left mine. He was back, and he called me "O."

Why had I ever hated that?

I ran my fingers over his dirt-streaked face. I took his scraped and bleeding hands and turned them over to examine them. He had the beginnings of his black eye that made me cringe. I brushed hair from his forehead, revealing a lump, and he winced. I pulled my hand away.

Oscar nudged my thigh. "Oh, Oscar." I ran my hand over his muddy coat. "Did you bring Brian back?"

Brian exhaled. "He saved my life."

I waited for him to say more, but he just stared at the cabin. I stood and helped him up, then draped his arm over my shoulder, and we limped to the porch. We climbed the steps, and he favored his left foot.

I opened the door, and he limped into the cabin. He jerked to a halt. "What's he doing here?"

I glanced at Perry. "Aaron shot him. I had to get him off the cold ground and treat his leg."

"Aaron shot him?" He shook his head. "You've

been busy, haven't you."

"You have no idea." We crossed the room to the fireplace, and I held his hand as he sat in the chair. He needed a blanket, so I dashed to the first bedroom. Three heavy blankets sat folded on a bed. I grabbed one and rushed back to Brian who was struggling to pull off his sweater. I helped him, my fingers brushing against his smooth skin.

I shivered and pushed all thought from my mind as I settled him in the chair next to the fire. I pulled off his soaked shoes and socks.

His lips were blue, and his teeth chattered. "We have no choice now. We have to stay."

"I know." I draped a blanket over his shoulders and knelt in front of him. There was blood on his sock. "You're bleeding?"

He sat forward and let the blanket settle around him, then plopped back in the chair. "It happened during the fall." He winced, and I tucked the edges of the blanket around him. "It's okay now. I can't feel it anymore."

"Oh." Was that a good thing, medically speaking?

I made a mental list of reasons why he couldn't feel his ankle, a break, lack of circulation, the cold. I was pretty sure that whatever the reason, it wasn't okay. I grabbed a mug from the kitchen and poured out some hot water.

"Here." I stepped over Oscar, who had sprawled in front of the fire, and handed the cup to Brian. He wrapped his fingers around the mug and put it to his lips.

"It's just water, but it's warm."

He sipped and sank back with a sigh, cradling the mug in dirty hands, his fingernails torn and bleeding.

"How did you get off that ledge?" I stared at him. I

wanted to know, but did he want to talk about it?

"I…" He croaked and took another sip, then choked.

I put a hand on his shoulder. "You're exhausted. This can wait."

He closed his eyes and sank back into the chair. I put another log on the fire and went to the kitchen, grabbed a dish towel, and rushed out to the porch railing. I made a snowball with the slush and wrapped the towel around it. I closed the door behind me, trapping the warmth inside.

I knelt beside him. "Here." I placed the snow-filled towel on his ankle, and he sighed.

I winced and glanced at a clock on the mantel, 1:32. It had been forty-eight minutes since we'd both jumped to avoid getting run over. It seemed like days. I glanced at him, but his eyes were closed, and the regular rise and fall of his chest assured me he slept.

Rest. He needed it.

Oscar had stretched out in front of the fireplace, melting snow puddling onto the floor around him. I grabbed some kitchen towels, and he let me rub him down, groaning and licking my hands as I worked around the scrapes in his thick fur. Whatever they'd done to get home left them both exhausted.

****

A viselike grip squeezed my heart as I sat staring at Brian's sleeping form. He had to be okay and so did Oscar. I had soup heating on the grate for when he woke. I threw another log on the fire, and soon the flames had the soup boiling.

Brian opened an eye and adjusted himself in the chair, wincing as he jostled his ankle. I pulled the dripping towel off his ankle. Had we stopped the swelling? I lifted the hem of his jeans to find purple skin, red and swollen. What could I do that I hadn't already done?

I'd had a sprained ankle before, but this could be broken. More ice? Maybe later. I tossed the towel in the sink and poured soup into a mug. I offered it to Brian.

He took it and sipped with his eyes closed. I went to pour some for Perry. I sank beside him on my haunches and offered him the cup, but he pushed my hand away. I rose to my feet. What more could I do? What would Emma do? I wrung my hands.

I turned to Brian. "You all right?"

Really? Did he look all right, Olivia?

"Hmmm," Brian mumbled.

Did that mean "yes"? I sipped my soup and took in every cut and abrasion on Brian's face and hands. What did the rest of him look like? I glanced away as heat rose to my cheeks.

Don't go there.

I sighed. The kiss made everything awkward now, or was it just me? The last thing on his mind was—

He had to be okay. That's all I cared about, but how did I make him okay, and care for Perry too? Brian mumbled something and held out the mug. I took it, his fingers brushing mine, and a jolt ran through me. The dimple in his chin was coated with stubble and dirt, and his jaw clenched as he repositioned his leg.

Aspirin. That might help. I rushed to the kitchen and opened one cabinet after another until, bingo. I pulled the bottle off the shelf and shook out three pills, then refilled Brian's cup with water.

"Here. Take these." I put the cup in his hand, and he swallowed the aspirin, then set the cup on the side table and stretched, his eyes already drooping. I brought a cup of water and some aspirin to Perry, but again he pushed my hand away.

The snow fell outside, and I scanned the room. I needed my journal, but I'd lost it in the first encounter with Perry and Aaron. I glared at Perry. Writing had helped calm me after Grandpa Billy died, and I could really use some calm right now. I glanced at Brian as he closed his eyes and settled in the chair.

What was I supposed to do now? I closed my eyes and pushed away the helplessness that threatened to swallow me whole.

****

The fire snapped, and I jerked, opening my eyes. I'd dozed. I glanced at Brian who sat watching me. My stomach flipped. Why? Why did my stomach flip? Why did my heart race? I didn't understand anything anymore. I glanced at Grandpa Billy's watch. I'd slept ten minutes.

He raised his leg and winced, pushing himself to the edge of the chair. "I need to…"

"Need to—" I stood. "Oh…"

He held out his hand. "Yes." His cheeks turned scarlet. "I need to go outside." One eye was swollen shut, and the other side of his face was bruised and scraped.

He struggled to stand but plopped back in the chair.

Outside? How was that going to happen?

He struggled to stand again, and I grabbed his arm, holding him steady. He ground his teeth as he hobbled one step.

"Thanks," he mumbled out of swollen lips.

My vision blurred. I sniffed and wiped my nose on my sleeve.

"I can do this." He pushed me away and took a step to the door. I reached my hand to his shoulder but didn't touch him. I wasn't sure where he was bruised and where he wasn't.

I moved to follow him, but he shook his head and opened the door with a grunt. He glanced at me with his swollen eyes and pulled the door closed behind him. He didn't want my help, and I didn't have a clue how to help him anyway without embarrassing us both.

Oscar snored on his rug by the fire, his legs twitched. Was he reliving the nightmare of his fall? I stared at the couch. Perry hadn't moved since I covered him with the blanket. Shouldn't he drink something?

Brian returned, opening the front door, and a blast of cold air hit me. I took his arm. He seemed so fragile. I helped him hobble to the chair by the fire. I wanted to ask him about the fall but held my tongue. He needed a long, healing sleep too, so my questions would have to wait.

His breath grew regular, so I put on my coat and boots and eased out the back door. I stood in the carport and stared at the melting snow. What a mess. Brian wouldn't be able to walk through that, and I wouldn't last long. Top Hat was lame, and Perry couldn't move, and I couldn't carry him. How did this happen? We needed help, but where would it come from?

"Come on, goddesses." I shook my fists at the sky. Top Hat nickered.

I walked around the cabin to the stall and held out my hand to him. Top Hat snorted and shook his head. I ran my fingers over his soft muzzle and lost myself in the reflection of his eyes.

Chapter Twenty

Smoke rose from the embers in the fireplace and filtered the sunshine that filled the living room. I glanced out the window. The snow had stopped. We could leave.

Oscar sniffed and growled by the front door.

"Did you wake me?" I clamped a hand over my mouth and glanced at Brian. His regular breathing didn't change.

Was this normal? He must need this sleep, right?

The back of my neck tensed. Why couldn't I snap my fingers and be home in Cedarville where I wasn't in charge of anything, where Mrs. Z kept the order and fussed over us? She must be frantic by now.

Wait. How long had I slept? What day was it? I turned my wrist and twisted the watch. 2:18? It was the fifteenth, and I'd missed my birthday party, big-time.

Oscar whined to be let out, and Brian opened his eyes. I waited for him to speak, but he just sat staring into the fire with vacant eyes.

I had to say something. I blurted, "You need a doctor, and so does Perry. He's going to die of infection if we don't do something."

Why did I say that?

Brian pushed himself from the chair and hobbled to a window, pulling back the curtain. I put a hand to my stomach as it tightened into a knot. Did I make him feel guilty? What was going through his mind?

This wasn't his fault.

He stared into the snowy yard. "We need to get to Franklin."

"We?" My legs wobbled, and I grabbed the back of the chair. "You can't walk. You could ride, but Top Hat pulled up lame when he was chasing Oscar. Besides, we don't know how far it is to Franklin."

Neither one of them would make it to Franklin, and I couldn't shake this fatigue. Was it the bursts of adrenaline from earlier that wore me out? I couldn't get sick again, not now.

Brian gazed down the driveway. "We have to try."

"Brian." I frowned. "Your ankle. You can't even walk."

"It doesn't matter."

I crossed the room to stand beside him. "Stupid Brewsters. This is their fault." I glanced at Perry, but he slept through what I'd said. I pressed my fingers to my temples. If I didn't leave soon, it could be too late for him.

"Are you okay?" he mumbled through swollen lips.

I frowned and clenched my fists. "I'll be fine. I'm worried about you and Perry."

His eyes softened, and my tension eased a bit. He sank into a kitchen chair.

"I have known the Brewsters since second grade, but in all that time, I never really knew them." He arched an eyebrow at me. "They are lost souls."

"Lost souls?" I stared at him.

"I'm worried about them."

"Of course." He never gave up on people.

"Something must have happened after their mom

died."

"But what?" How did Brian do this? Find a way to turn the Brewsters from monsters into humans. Did that make me petty and small-minded? *Yes.*

I sank into the chair beside him. "So, what do we do?"

"You might have to go to Franklin alone. It could be our only hope to save Perry, and you'll have to leave before another storm hits."

"And you. What about you?" I closed my eyes, the staccato beat of snow melting from the roof grated on my nerves like Chinese water torture. A mist rose from every surface of the yard, moisture lifted into the air to form steam clouds. The lead ball in my stomach had moved to my head, which was not big enough to hold a lead ball.

I frowned at Brian. "You know, this is Samson's fault. He should have gone to Franklin himself. The Brewsters wouldn't have bothered him. We're just kids." I jumped from my chair and paced the room. Why did I blame the Brewsters and Samson? Wasn't part of this my fault? I was the one who led us here. My eyes ached, and I clenched my teeth. "This is such a mess."

"Yeah, this crackling fire is a total mess, so is this cabin filled with food and blankets. You're right." Brian shook his head.

I stared at him. He cocked an eyebrow at me, and I deflated like a birthday balloon. "You know what I mean."

Brian grimaced, but his puffed eyes held a twinkle, and his cracked lips turned up at the corners. He'd followed me to Silver Springs Stable, and I pushed him away, then he followed me to Cedar Hills, then into the mountains, and even when Old Charlie ran off, he kept following me. He'd never left me alone, and that meant something. Did I want it to mean something? I sighed and touched my lips. His kiss had changed everything. I needed him. He made me a better person, made me want to help Mr. G, Gracie, and Perry.

I wiped my forehead with a shaky hand. "Guess I'll get ready, then."

"Take the gun if you're worried about Aaron."

I frowned. "Worried about Aaron? I'm more worried about you and Perry."

"Go to the clinic, then go to the police."

Perry moaned, and I gasped.

He was awake, which meant—

He stared into the fire. A nerve in my neck pinched, and I rubbed the sore spot. Did I want to go to the police? I did when Brian said it, but now that Perry was awake…

Did I still care for him? I frowned and glared at Brian. "Why does everything have to be so difficult?"

I pushed my feet into my boots and arms into my jacket, zipped, and opened the door. Top Hat reached his nose to me. "Sorry, Top Hat, you don't get to go to Franklin." I smoothed my hand over his glossy forehead.

Brian emerged from the house with my backpack and held it out to me.

"You shouldn't be up."

"I wish I could go with."

I shrugged into the pack. Top Hat tossed his head. He wanted to go too, but neither of them would make it. I had to go alone.

"Be careful." Pain had etched wrinkles around his eyes and mouth.

"I'll be back before you know it." I read the watch, 2:55.

I ducked through the drips melting off the roof, my rubber riding boots saving me from the slush I'd have to walk through. How many miles to Franklin? I glanced over my shoulder. Brian waved, then disappeared into the cabin and closed the door. The temperature seemed to drop ten degrees.

Top Hat pawed at the door as if to say, "Take me with you."

I trudged down the driveway. I refused to turn around. Instead, I stared into the mountains, the sound of rushing water filling the air. A tremor shook my body.

****

Brian stared out the window as Olivia disappeared down the driveway. Snow melted off the eaves, drip, drip, drip. He hobbled the length of the cabin. Perry tracked him with his eyes as he paced. This was torture times two, ankle and heart.

What was it about Perry that made her care?

Brian glared at his rival. Olivia had always pushed him away at every chance. Was she slipping away from him before he could change her mind? Perry had abandoned her after his mom's funeral, and she'd disappeared into her bedroom for days crying over this jerk. What could he do about Perry? Brian grabbed the back of the chair for support and plopped into the cushion. Who would she choose?

He sighed and gazed out the window. If it hadn't been for Mrs. Z, he wouldn't even be here. She'd arrived too late to save his parents, but Trevor, who was next door, had helped her transport him somewhere so she could care for him.

He sighed. Those events blurred together with the nightmare of losing his parents and all the other nightmares. Then the dreams changed and became light and filled with hope, but he never dreamed he'd wake up in Olivia's house.

He rubbed his ankle. Was it broken or just sprained? Why did he have to fall off the cliff? He needed to go to Franklin with her, but did she want him to? Sure, she did. She'd let him kiss her, and she'd kissed him back, right?

He glanced at Perry, who clenched his teeth and shifted under the blanket. The pain must be unbearable.

Brian jabbed a finger at Perry. "You started this."

Perry turned his head toward the back of the couch. Brian limped to the couch and lifted the blanket. She hadn't wrapped it. Brian stepped back. How did you wrap something that torn and bloody?

"That good, huh?" Perry's voice caught him off guard.

"It could be better." Should he tell him it was going to get infected? Why? There wasn't anything he could do to stop it.

But he had to do something, right? He hobbled to the bathroom and opened the medicine cabinet. Alcohol. He lifted the bottle and grabbed a towel from the shelf, then limped back to the couch using the furniture and the walls for support.

"I'll just say I'm sorry now." He opened the bottle, and holding the towel under his leg, he poured.

"Mother fu—" Perry sat and reached for his leg. "Agh. What the…"

Brian pressed his shoulder, and Perry groaned, collapsing into the pillow.

Brian glared at Perry. "You know where you are, right?"

Perry gritted his teeth and nodded. "I was shot in the

leg, not the head."

"Your brother ran off after he shot you, and Olivia dragged you inside by herself."

Perry closed his eyes. "I do know that. Hurt like hell getting up those back steps."

Brian dabbed at the wound to dry it.

"Stop." Perry winced and pushed Brian's hands away.

If help didn't arrive soon...*Don't even think it.*

Brian stood and crossed his arms. "Olivia left for Franklin."

Perry opened his eyes. "You let her leave by herself? You realize Aaron is still out there."

Brian cleared his throat. Did Perry still care about her? "You should have thought of her before you came here to steal Top Hat."

"You think I can control Aaron? I came with him to stop him from hurting her." Perry tried to sit.

"You what?" Brian glared at Perry.

"Agh." He gripped his wounded leg. "Dude, there's got to be aspirin here, right?"

Brian hobbled to the kitchen. Where had Olivia found that bottle? Above the sink? He couldn't wrap his mind around what Perry had said.

"So, are you saying you came to save us? You have a funny way of showing it." Brian opened the bottle and shook three into his palm. "Here." He held out the pills and a glass of water.

Perry put them in his mouth and drank them down. He settled back on the couch. "Aaron is out of control. Since Mom..."

Brian hung his head. He hadn't expected Perry to be so rational. What did he know about this guy anyway?

159

He cleared his throat. "Yeah. We all lost people."

Perry scoffed. "We did. In more ways than one. All Dad does now is drink. He disappeared a week ago. Did you know that? And Aaron had to blame someone for Mom's death, right? He always did have a temper, but after Dad disappeared, he started going on tirades, and I had to go with him to stop him from doing too much damage. He needs more help than I can give him, and with Dad gone—" Perry ran his hand along his thigh and grimaced.

Brian unclenched his fists. "You think I believe your excuses?" He took a step and grimaced. He needed aspirin too, probably surgery, but that wasn't going to happen any time soon. He dropped into a chair, clenching his fists.

Perry shook his head and chuckled. "The Brewster brothers. We strike fear into the hearts of any in our path." He rubbed his eyebrow with a finger and glanced at Brian. "Does she hate me?"

"What?" Brian frowned. Olivia hating Perry was all he'd hoped for since she started dating this jerk, but now that he was learning more about this guy, he didn't know what to say. "I think she's given up on you. You left her, remember?"

"I'll never forget."

Brian closed his eyes. Was this how he lost her?

****

Josh rode in the back of the truck with Dad, Mark Blunt, Tucker Johnson, and his little brother Stevie. Five experienced rescue team members, and he was nervous. Why? They'd left Dr. Johnson and Emma at Samson's. Dad had charged into the house, and the whole crew could hear everything he said. Josh wished he could see

Samson's face.

Barb came outside dabbing at her eyes and waved at the rescue team, with Emma by her side, as the truck pulled away from the house.

He chewed his lip. She had the knack of caring for people suffering both physical and mental anguish.

She couldn't even take care of herself when he met her, but she healed in record speed and began helping him when she could. Now Cedarville needed her as much as he did. The truck chugged uphill, the muffler long gone. Virg steered around downed trees, and the dogs ran alongside the truck, panting.

A foul odor filled the air, and one by one, the dogs stopped and sniffed around the brush at the side of the road. Dad stood up in the bed of the truck and pounded on the cab roof three times.

"Stop the truck, Virg."

The brakes squealed as the truck came to a full stop, and Dad jumped out.

"Something die?" Virg leaned out the window.

"That's what we're going to find out." Dad strode after the dogs. "Come on, boys."

Tucker jumped out the back with Stevie, and they followed the dogs into the underbrush. Tucker put a hand over his mouth and nose and held up his other hand. He turned. "It's a man." He shook his head.

He jogged back to the truck. "We got a body, Virg."

Tucker helped Stevie gather the dogs, and Dad returned to lean against the truck.

Virg frowned. "A body? It's not—"

"Not Brian." He finished for him.

"It's Frank Brewster. I'd know that jean jacket anywhere." Stevie sighed. "Wild animals got to him, so it's not clear what killed him."

"Probably drink." Tucker gazed over the body into the forest. "How he ended up here is the sixty-four-dollar question."

"That changes our plans, guys. We need to gather his remains and get them to the county morgue." Dad glanced at Virg as he opened the truck door.

"It's only right." Josh helped Virg pull a blue tarp from behind the seat. He released the tarp, and Josh bundled it in his arms. Dad waited for Stevie to tether the dog. Then Virg followed him into the brush. Josh brought up the rear with the tarp.

Tucker held his hat in his hands. "Not many will shed a tear for Frank, but my question is, where are Aaron and Perry?"

Josh gazed into the mountains. Would they find the boys alive?

Chapter Twenty-One

Light snowflakes fell as I hunched into the wind, the snow finding the gap between my neck and the hood. I rounded a bend in the road, and the temperature seemed to drop. I was climbing in altitude, but steeper? Really?

The branches hung low weighed down by snow, and my footsteps crunched as I plodded on. I peered into the branches. A green sign showed through the trees at the side of the road.

ENTERING FRANKLIN

"I made it." I stumbled and laughed and spun around. Where was the town? I put one foot in front of the other and peered into the falling flakes. A house appeared as if an apparition. It was right here all this time.

We might have braved the storms if we'd had a crystal ball. I put a hand to my wrist. 6:12. I'd been on the road for almost three hours, and I'd made it before dark. Win, win.

I turned onto a deserted street lined with shops. Smoke rose from some of the houses, but no one came out to check on the stranger walking through town in a snowstorm. The chalet-style architecture gave Franklin a quaint, old-world charm, but I shivered. Were people watching me from behind their curtains?

I strode down the street to a building with a sign that

read "Clinic." I walked up the porch and climbed the steps to the front door of the clinic. Fatigue hit me like a wall. All I wanted was sleep. I closed my eyes and sent up a silent prayer before turning the knob.

Locked. My knees buckled. How could it be locked? The snow had been shoveled from the steps, so someone was here. I turned to walk down the steps when the door cracked, and a woman gasped. I stumbled, and she reached out and took my arm. She led me inside.

"I'm Dr. Nordby. Where did you—"

I glanced at her, but no words came.

"Lilli?" she called over her shoulder. "I need you?"

I wanted to thank her, but my throat had closed.

A short stocky woman appeared, shrugging into a jacket. "What's up?" Her boots clattered on the floor as she bustled down the hall to join us.

"I'll need your help with this young lady."

Dr. N was brisk and efficient, I'd give her that. She led me down a hallway and sat me in a room. She handed me a glass of water. I drank it down, and she filled it again. I sipped and set the glass on the counter. I pulled my hood off as she stood waiting.

"I thought you were in Yakima?" I took in the sparse clean room, the antiseptic aroma that permeated the place. I'd hit the jackpot. A fit of coughing shook my body, and I reached for the glass.

They needed to know about Brian and Perry. "We have to—" I tilted sideways.

"Lilli, grab her other arm. Let's get her settled in a room."

Lilli's frown unsettled me. "She's sick? But that means we can't—"

"Lilli." Dr. N shook her head. "Let's get her on the

164

couch, and we can discuss that later."

"But Cedarville needs—"

Was I missing something?

"Lilli. One thing at a time." Dr. N helped me onto a couch. "Sorry. This is the closest thing to a bed in the clinic."

I tried to sit. "No." I needed to tell her something, but what was it? Dr. N pressed me back against the pillow. "I need to get back."

"You need water." She left and returned a moment later. "Here." She raised my head, and I sipped, then choked.

"I shouldn't be sick," I croaked as she helped me remove my coat.

"This is a novel virus." Dr. N sighed. "We don't have any immunity to this. In fact, some waterborne pathogens can negatively impact the immune system and make a person sicker." Dr. Nordby untied my boots and slipped them from my feet. Lilli returned. Dr. N smiled. "Lilli, prepare a dose, five drops in hot water." The door clicked as she left.

She placed a warm hand on my shoulder. "Now, tell me where you have to get back to?"

"The cabin." Why was I so weak? I'd walked down the street five minutes ago, and now I couldn't lift my head off the pillow. I was sick again.

Not funny, Universe.

"There are people at the cabin?" She frowned at me.

I tried to sit. "Perry and Brian are hurt. We must ge—"

She pressed me back, and I relaxed onto the couch, dizziness and nausea making the room spin. I was sick, but when had it started? Who was I kidding. This had been coming on since before Perry had been shot, since I'd left the house two days ago. I'd never fully recovered. The door opened, and a warm hand helped me raise my head, and a warm cup holding a fragrant drink was held to my lips. I drank it down.

I floated back on the pillow. It was hitting me too fast, and the sensation like a swirling feather in a whirlpool sucked me farther and farther down the funnel. I fought against it, trying to explain that Brian and Perry needed—

****

A blizzard raged outside the window. I wanted to scream. Would this snow ever end? I had to get back. I pushed my legs over the side of the couch and sat. I stared out the window. I couldn't see two feet beyond the glass. I gasped. Why was the snow pink? What would cause that? Sunset?

Voices came from down the hall. Dr. Nordby and Lilli were talking about me, and Lilli was crying. Pink snow, Lilli crying, what was going on? I stood, but my legs wouldn't work. If I could only get to the door, step into the hall, but my feet were glued to the floor, my head full of sawdust.

I fell back into bed and reached for Grandpa Billy's watch. It wasn't on my wrist. Top Hat nickered in the waiting room, but what was he doing here? He should be at the cabin. I rose from the bed and floated down the hall and opened the front door. I ran outside in my bare feet. Brian would be so angry at me, sick and barefoot in the snow.

I gazed across the street at a house, but instead of snow, the lawn was green with grass. Mount Rainier shone in the distance, but the pink snow had disappeared.

Where'd it go?

I ran into the cabin, but the fire was out. Had Brian left with Perry? Did they find their way to Cedarville with the medicine? I opened the back door and stopped in my tracks. Shadow stood in the stall.

"Shadow?" I reached out a hand to her, and she nickered. I ran to her, threw my arms around her neck. Had Mr. G lied? I ran my hands over her warm neck and withers. I lifted her mane and inhaled her wonderful, horsey perfume. I closed my eyes. Was I at Silver Springs Stable?

No. This must be a dream.

Grandpa Billy had mumbled about Grandma and his farm. He must have gone through a dream state, too. He'd spoken gibberish right to the end.

I had never had such vivid dreams, not like this, so real. With a jolt, the emptiness in my chest throbbed—Shadow, Mom, Dad, Grandpa Billy. Gone. I ached to hold them all in my arms. I fell back in the pillows.

I wasn't afraid to die.

****

I fluttered my eyes open. Lilli held my hand and squeezed my fingers.

"She's awake." She sat on the edge of the bed. "You were crying out in your sleep."

Was this part of the dream too? Dr. N rushed in with her crinkly eyed smile. I opened my mouth to speak, but I croaked, my throat as dry as dust.

"This is a good sign." Dr. Nordby smiled. "Can you speak?"

"Water." I placed a hand over my mouth.

Lilli grabbed a glass of water off the nightstand. I drank it down.

I glanced out the window at the white yard. "The cabin. My friends…"

I tried to sit, but my whole body hurt. Lilli took my hand as Dr. N took my temperature and blood pressure.

"What did you give me?"

Dr. Nordby frowned. "It's not a cure, but it helps your body heal itself. We were just preparing to leave for Cedarville when the storm hit, and then you arrived." She smiled and stood with her hands on her hips. She was tall and slender, like Mom.

I ran my hands over my face. "I feel better, but the dreams…" Sleep threatened to drag me back down, but I wouldn't let it. "Perry's been shot, and I'm pretty sure Brian broke his ankle. They need you. Today."

She held her hands up as if to stop a train, which would be me and my motormouth.

She smiled down at me. "We will help them, but we can't go anywhere until this snow subsides." She put a hand on my shoulder. "It seemed like you were dreaming."

I nodded. She sank into a chair beside the couch, her eyes bright and kind.

"Lucid dreams are part of the healing process for some reason. While we're waiting, perhaps you can tell me about yours?" She pulled a pen and notepad from her pocket and sat, ready to take notes.

"Oh." I rubbed my eyes and glanced at the watch. 9:44.

I scanned the room, my gaze landing on Dr. N. What kind of doctor was she, asking about dreams? At least it wasn't a nightmare. My dreams had changed on this trip, and if telling her about them would get her to help Brian and Perry, I'd tell her anything she wanted to hear.

I scratched my head, the images emerging. I closed my eyes. "It was…weird. There was pink snow, and Shadow was alive. Then there was green grass in front of the cabin." Lilli handed me the glass again, and I emptied it.

"That's enough for now." Dr. N dropped the pen and pad in her pocket and smiled down at me. "Rest, sleep if you can." She rose to leave.

"Shall I stay?" Lilli took my hand.

I nodded and held her hand as I drifted into darkness.

Chapter Twenty-Two

Brian lifted the curtain and stared into the blizzard. Olivia was out there somewhere—alone. Did she make it to Franklin before dark? He rubbed the bridge of his nose. Of course, she made it. She was stubborn, independent, and driven when she had a goal. She could take care of herself. He'd seen her do it, and besides, she had the gun.

But did she make it to Franklin?

Perry moaned from the couch. Brian moved to his side. "Water?" Perry pushed the covers down to his waist, his eyebrows pinched into a straight line on his brow. Brian took a glass from the coffee table and held it to Perry.

Perry pushed it away. "Not water. Why'd you let her leave?" Perry opened his eyes to mere slits and glared at Brian. "She's alone out there, and you…" A fit of coughing shook his body, and he winced.

Brian took a step back, a jolt of guilt running through him like electricity. Who was he to scold Brian for not taking care of Olivia?

Brian clenched his fists. "I had no choice. You've met her, right?"

Maybe he could just punch Perry once, hard, right in the face, and get it over with? He slumped his shoulders. No. What would that solve?

He sighed. "She's gone to get the doctor for you, remember? Did you forget you're shot and wounded? It must be affecting your ability to think straight." He muttered under his breath. "Obviously."

"I heard that."

Perry lifted the blanket and exposed the wound. It was red and swollen, with no signs of discharge yet. Brian winced. It had to hurt, but did he clean it, leave it alone?

"I better clean it." He limped to the kitchen counter and returned with the alcohol and another towel.

Perry closed his eyes. "Do you know what you're doing? Because last time—"

"This will hurt." He poured alcohol on the wound.

"God damn, motherfucker, shit, shit, shit." Perry grabbed his leg above and below the wound. He hissed with his eyes clamped shut. "I don't think you're supposed to pour alcohol right on an open wound, asshole." Perry's eyes teared, but he didn't cry.

Brian turned as he screwed the lid on the alcohol jar. Did Perry's pain bring him some sort of satisfaction? No. He wasn't an animal, but it soothed the jab Perry had taken. Yes, O was out there, alone, but she'd had to go, right? He lowered himself into the chair by the fireplace and pulled up his pant leg. His ankle puffed over his boot top. He cringed. He had left his boot on because he'd never get it back on if he had removed it. How could he help Olivia like this?

He stood using the chair for support and hobbled to the window, the snow a maddening swirl of white.

****

Dr. Nordby was standing over me, holding my wrist as I came to consciousness. I ran my tongue over the roof of my dry mouth, and she ran the thermometer over my forehead. Had she been standing there waiting for me to wake up? If so, I should thank her. The thermometer beeped, and I stared at her so absorbed in her work.

Brian and Perry needed this doctor. She was amazing. I stared at her, so confident, helping me in a real way, one that produced results. This was what I wanted to do. I wanted to help people, like she did. She read the thermometer and grunted, jotting a note on her pad. I reached my hand to my head as she slipped the thermometer in her pocket and focused her gaze on me.

"You are recovering faster than I expected." She smiled down at me. "How do you feel?"

"Like we need to leave so we can help my friends." I couldn't shake my dread for Perry and Brian. I sat and pushed stray hairs behind my ears. "When can we, leave I mean?"

"Leave? You still need rest. Besides, the storm is raging outside. We can't leave until first light, snow or no snow." She held my chart for one more glance. "Yours is the fastest recovery I've seen yet." She smiled, and her eyes crinkled at the corners like Mom's.

Why had I made that comparison? I cleared my throat. She wanted to hear about dreams, right? So, I'd give her dreams. Anything to pass the time.

"I had such strange dreams. What did you call them? Lucid?"

"Mmhmm." She nodded. "You mumbled something about a journal. Do you keep a journal?"

"I do. My boy— A friend gave it to me, but I lost it on the road somewhere trying to get here." I frowned at her. What else had I mumbled in my nightmare-riddled sleep?

"That's unfortunate. Did you write about your dreams as you were recovering from novel HAV? That would really help my research." She opened a drawer and handed me a little blue book with a paper cover like the kind we used in school for exams. "Do you remember any of your dreams from that time? Maybe you could write them down for me?"

I shrugged. "I can, but why?"

"The dreams seem to be linked to recovery. People who survive have all had lucid dreams, and I'm looking for the connection."

"Why would dreams help?"

"I'm not sure, but maybe there is a psychological connection. In a nutshell, I'm finding that survivor's guilt has affected many of my patients, causing a depression. It seems that our psyches can help us heal, but only if we want to survive. The herbal tincture I've developed heals the liver and also helps with depression, but there's a psychological connection between the dreams and healing that provides an added boost."

I didn't know what to say. I had wanted to stay in the dream with Shadow, Mom, Dad, and Grandpa Billy forever, but a sense of unfinished business had pulled me back. I bit my lower lip. I had ridden Shadow in one, kissed Perry in another, and lay in Brian's arms in another…

Heat rose from my neck to my cheeks and forehead. "Some of them are personal." Brian's eyes haunted me. I'd left him alone with Perry. How was that going?

Dr. N nodded. "That's normal. I'm more interested in the energy you felt during the dream, whether it was positive or negative? That way you don't have to get too specific about the details of the dream. Does that help?"

A familiar itch started behind my eyes, and I rubbed them. "How long before we can leave?"

"Did you forget already? We can't leave until morning." She put a hand on mine. "How long did it take you to get here?"

"A couple of hours all uphill." I turned my head to the window. Light from the candle reflected off the glass, and the smell of wax filled the room.

"Good news, then. Downhill will take less time, but you need more rest anyway. Besides, we had everything ready to go before you arrived, so we can leave at sunrise which is around seven o'clock." She smiled as she stepped out of the room, closing the door behind her.

I slumped back into the pillow and held up the watch. 12:16 a.m. It was the sixteenth. Could I wait seven hours to leave? Did I have a choice?

****

Voices filtered into my sleep, and I yawned. Where was I? Franklin. I'd made it. Was it morning? It must be. The voices made sense now. Dr. N and Lilli were preparing to leave, and I was still in bed. I twisted the watch so I could read it. 6:32. Light was seeping into the room, but it wasn't fully light out yet.

A bowl of water sat on the counter in the stark room. I swung my feet to the floor and stood waiting for the dizziness to pass, but I wasn't dizzy. What a relief. What was I waiting for? I walked to the water and splashed it on my face. I wiped myself dry with a washcloth, then scrubbed my arms and legs, easing the ache from my body. We had to get to Brian and Perry before infection—

They were so different, but I dreamed of them both. Perry had broken my heart, though, so Brian should be my choice, right? Grandpa had never liked Perry, and that meant something, right? Brian…

Who cared if he was younger? He'd changed overnight, or had I never paid attention? Maybe he had been changing all along, especially his biceps…

Quit it, O.

I dressed and padded down the hall in stockinged feet. "Where are my boots?" I scanned the waiting room.

"Beside the fireplace." Lilli pointed.

Lilli and Dr. Nordby murmured together as I pulled my riding boots. They shrugged into full packs. I grabbed mine, and frigid air hit my face as I stepped out the front door. The fresh air hit me like a soft cushion. I filled my lungs and exhaled, a smile forming on my lips.

I had made it to Franklin. I had found the doctor, and she had the meds. It was a minor miracle, right? I rubbed my fingers together for warmth.

"You okay?" Dr. N joined me on the porch. She reached out her hand to place it on my forehead.

"I'm ready to go." I wobbled. "I got this."

She followed and stood near as I clomped down the steps. Did she think I was going to fall over? I sat on the bottom step as she helped me fasten the snowshoes, but all the while, I wanted to scream for her to hurry. Would Perry still be alive when we got there? Would Brian? I had an urgent need to be on the road back to the cabin.

"Ready?" Dr. Nordby tightened the straps on her snowshoes. "Where's Lilli?"

****

Brian stood over Perry, who lay on the couch thrashing and mumbling in his sleep. He had a fever and kept pushing the blanket off. It had probably been a rough night for him with the pain and all. His leg must be killing him, but his nightmares weren't helping.

Where was Olivia? How could he sleep not knowing if she made it or if she was lying by the side of the road, covered in snow? Was she on her way back with the doctor? Had she even made it to Franklin? He sighed and rubbed his ankle. It throbbed. What would she do if the doctor couldn't save Perry? What if he was an invalid with a permanent limp?

"Morning, asshole."

Brian clenched his fists. "Bring it."

Perry glared at him.

He took in a lungful of air and released it. "Look. We are stuck here together, so we might as well be civil." Perry was in pain. How did he reason with someone who was borderline delusional?

"Civil? You stole my girl."

Was he delirious? "You idiot. You blew it, and you know it. She'll never go back to you. She's…"

"She's what? Yours now?" He smirked.

"Hmm." Brian hobbled to the kitchen and pulled the bottle of aspirin from the shelf. "Here. You need something for the pain." He offered Perry three, with a sip of water. With any luck, they'd let him sleep until O arrived with the doctor.

He took two for himself and dropped into a chair by the fire. He lifted his ankle onto the coffee table and hissed air through his teeth. What was the acronym? RICE? Rest, Ice, Compress, and Elevate. He should have had Olivia help him wrap it before she left, but with all the chaos of him falling off a cliff and Perry getting shot, no one was thinking straight.

He yawned. Rest and Elevate would have to suffice until Olivia returned. The aspirin relaxed him, and he drifted from one thought to another. *Had she made it? Was she thinking of him? When would she…"*

****

A light snow fell as I trudged after Lilli and Dr. N. I brushed a flake from my face. The sky was bright behind the thin cloud cover. Did that mean the snow would stop soon? I rubbed my hands together to get the blood flowing. The crash of a door opening stopped me.

A man ran toward us from one of the houses, his eyes wide, a young boy racing behind him. "Dr. Nordby. Dr. Nordby." He skidded to a stop in front of us.

Now what? Didn't they understand that Dr. N was ready to leave? She was coming with me.

"Ma's burning up." The boy's words screeched from his lips in a plaintive wail.

"Martha?" Dr. N peered into the eyes of the man.

"We were all sleeping, and she woke crying about snakes in the bed. There ain't no snakes in the bed." He wrung his hands and shuffled his feet.

"Right." She put a hand on Lilli's shoulder. "You'll have to leave without me. I'll take care of this and catch up after."

"But?" Lilli's mouth dropped. "I—I—"

"You can do this. Just assess and treat what you can." She glanced at me and shook her head. "I can't leave until I've treated Martha. Now go." She turned to the man. "Hurry."

I stared after her, ready to object, but she was already halfway to a chalet-like home down the street.

Lilli gaped after Dr. N, oblivious to another woman holding a baby, who walked up to stand beside her. Lilli startled and placed a hand on the woman's shoulder.

"Jade. I didn't think you were going to make it."

177

Lilli kissed her lips as the baby gurgled in the bundle of blankets.

"Someone was a fussbudget." She leaned into Lilli who motioned to me with her hand.

"Olivia, this is my partner, Jade, and this little troublemaker is Ike."

"Trouble is his middle name." She adjusted the infant with one arm and held out her hand. I shook it, surprised by how warm it was in this frigid climate. "Lilli will take good care of your friends. She's top-notch, my Lil." Jade glowed and rocked Ike. He didn't stir.

I swallowed hard and choked out, "I'm just happy she can come." Was that true? I'd wanted the doctor. The jury was still out on Lilli, but Jade sure had confidence in her.

"Give me a minute." Lilli took Jade's hand and led her into an alley of sorts.

How long was a minute? Did I have a choice? No. Lilli was a take-charge kind of person. I liked that, but how long would it take to say goodbye?

I peered around the corner where Lilli stood holding Jade's hand. They sandwiched baby Ike between them, and he gurgled and squirmed. Every word they said seemed amplified by the confined space.

"It's the next step, hon." Lilli's voice carried even though she whispered. "I'll learn so much on this trip, and Cedarville—"

"I understand, but this takes you away from me? I don't like it." Jade's low voice came out like molasses with a slight twang like she was from the South. "And the house—"

So, was Jade lying? She didn't want Lilli to go, that was for sure. I scanned the street for Dr. N, but she'd disappeared into one of the houses. Maybe she'd join us by the time Lilli finished saying goodbye.

"I'll check out houses while I'm there. It will be perfect for us."

A twinge of guilt hit me. I shouldn't eavesdrop, but their voices echoed off the walls of the alley. Was Lilli the new doctor everyone was talking about? She seemed more like a nurse assistant.

"They know we have seven kids coming with us, right?"

Lilli sighed. "Yes, hon, they know about Ike." She leaned over and kissed the baby.

Jade leaned down, giving her a kiss, and I glanced away, heat rising to my cheeks. People kissed all the time, but this kiss lingered. Was that how Brian had kissed me? Why couldn't I stop obsessing over that? It was just a kiss, for goodness' sake.

Jade pulled away. "We'd better leave it at that, or you'll never get out of here." A chuckle rumbled deep in her chest.

I turned away and took a couple steps to the middle of the road. The last thing I wanted was to get caught snooping.

Lilli tightened her backpack straps. "Shall we?"

I nodded. "Everything okay?"

"Yep. Perfect." She turned to Jade. "I love you, babe."

I waved to Jade, and she raised a hand, her eyes twinkling. Lilli was lucky to have skills that saved people and Jade who loved her. I glanced over my shoulder when we rounded the corner out of town. Jade was still there, but her eyes were red rimmed.

Chapter Twenty-Three

I let gravity pull me down the mountain. With each step, I was getting closer to the cabin and Brian. Lilli followed on snowshoes. The snow crunched as I ran.

"Wait up."

I stopped and waited for Lilli to catch up. She glanced at me and then at the road. Was she nervous? Was I frowning? I tried to give her a reassuring smile, but my cheeks were frozen. I rubbed them with my hands. She caught up to me, and we stood in the middle of the road surrounded by alpine forest.

I had to break the silence between us. "Have you treated many gunshot wounds?" I had a right to ask, didn't I? Not like there was anyone else to help Perry, but still.

She cleared her throat, her face pale. "Once."

"Huh." I nodded. Was once good enough to help Perry?

She'd answered without pausing, though, so perhaps she was telling the truth. I'd be nervous too if I were sent to do a job I wasn't prepared for.

Wait. That's exactly what I was doing. Mr. G's job, then Samson's job, and now Cedarville's job.

I'd encountered elk and raccoons, blizzards, hypothermia, and the Brewsters, one of whom I'd locked lips with. What did I ever see in him?

I shuddered, then turned to trek down the mountain. Lilli had to keep up because it was more than gravity pulling me to the cabin, but what would I find when I got there?

****

Brian poured a glass of water and set it in front of Perry. He was done trying to get this stubborn son-of-a-whatever to drink.

Perry lifted the glass to his lips and guzzled it down, then spurted as he choked.

"Slow down." Brian pounded him on the back. Was that too hard? Did he care?

"When does Olivia get back?" Perry glanced at Brian, then winced and put a hand to his thigh. "My leg is throbbing."

"Your guess is as good as mine. All I can do is get you more aspirin." Brian leaned against the couch, favoring his ankle. "With any luck, you'll fall asleep again."

"You hate me. I get it, but…"

"But what? Huh? You and your brother come in here and threaten to take Top Hat or kill him trying? And when you can't take him, you threaten to hurt Olivia?" Brian pounded one fist into the other.

"To be fair, Aaron would have hurt you too." Perry glared at him.

Brian sighed. This conversation was going nowhere. "You need rest."

"The last thing I want is more sleep. I can't take the nightmares." Perry pushed up his sleeves.

Was he getting ready for a fight? Who did this guy think he was? Superman? Brian limped to the chair and sat. He glared at Perry.

"I couldn't sleep if I tried." Perry rubbed his thigh below the wound and grimaced.

"Fine, but watch your mouth, or you'll find my fist in it." Did he say that out loud? He was trying to rise above this but failing. Good thing O wasn't here.

"You like her." He stared into the fire. "Does she like you back?"

Was that remorse in his voice? Did Perry still care about Olivia? A twinge prickled at Brian's chest. Was Perry still a threat? Olivia wouldn't go back to this creep after everything he'd done, would she?

"How should I know. Olivia and I are out here helping people, and you are doing the opposite, destroying property, stealing, taking. What is wrong with you?" Brian clenched his teeth. He'd said too much, yet again.

"You're such a Boy Scout. That's what she called you when we were together, and Dorkmeister, don't forget that one." Perry sighed. "But you're right. After Mom—

"Then Dad—

"I stayed with my brother, and as I tried to tell you before, Aaron would have done those things with or without me. I tried to stop him, or at least make what he did less damaging, but I'm not his parent." He scrubbed his face with his hands, pain deepening the creases in his brow. "Why am I even telling you this? You'll never believe me." He let his hands drop into his lap. "You sent Olivia for the police, didn't you?"

"What if I did?" Brian turned to Perry and glared. "You'd say anything to save your own hide and your brother's, but I'm not buying a word of it."

Perry clamped his mouth shut, and Brian folded his

arms across his chest. Perry still had a thing for Olivia. Brian clenched his fists. What was it about Olivia that made him care so much? She had called him Dorkmeister, and still he'd kissed her. A knot tightened in his stomach. Had she laughed about that kiss all the way to Franklin?

****

The sky was gray, but at least it wasn't snowing. I glanced over my shoulder. Lilli dragged her snowshoes through the deep drifts, trying to catch up. I needed to get to Brian. And Perry. I stared into the distance. Which one was I rushing back to? Brian, right? Lilli huffed and puffed as she caught up to me.

"Did you write any dreams in the journal?"

Could she read my mind? Were my feelings for Brian clear to her? She'd never even met Brian. "My dreams are confusing. I don't know if I…"

Lilli pushed her hat back from her eyes. "Dr. Nordby just needs the emotions that come with the dream. Were you afraid, happy, sad? Were they colorful or in shades of gray?"

I gazed up at the sky, then at Lilli. "They were filled with love and longing, and everything seemed so real," I said. "Like the one where Shadow was alive. Her warmth and horse-scent filled my senses, then another where Mom and Dad…"

I shifted from foot to foot, my mind stuck on the dream of Mom. Was she reaching out from the grave? I'd bring her back if I could, but she was gone.

I had asked her if she were really dead. Who asked that, even in a dream? I could never take those words back. No. My dreams were too personal. They hurt. My cheeks burned but not from fever, thanks to Dr. Nordby's tincture. It was like magic.

Emily Dickinson's poem ran through my mind.

A WORD is dead
When it is said,
Some say.
I say it just
Begins to live
That day.

A word did begin to live as soon as you say it. A word could cause pain. We spoke words without thinking.

Perry's last words to me were that he didn't care. Sure, he'd said them at his mom's funeral when he was in shock with grief, but he'd thrown the words like stones, and they still weighed down my heart.

But what about his actions? I mean, he had tried to stop Aaron, who shot Perry with the rifle, but that was an accident, right? Perry didn't deserve to get shot. No one did. I sighed.

Perry had cried at his mom's funeral, but Aaron's eyes were slits, and his fists clenched and unclenched throughout the whole service. Their dad reeked of whisky and slurred his words. Hadn't he disappeared? Where would he go, and why would he leave his boys, and why had no one helped them like Mrs. Z had done for Brian and me? They didn't have anyone who cared.

I sighed. This all began because I needed to find out if Shadow lived, to get out of Cedarville and away from Mrs. Z and Brian. Then Mr. G needed help and sent us to Samson, and Samson needed help, and then Perry needed help, and Brian too.

I crunched through the fresh snow. If I could only get back to Cedarville in one piece, I'd kiss Mrs. Z and appreciate the life I'd have to live without Grandpa Billy, Mom, or Dad.

Lilli coughed, and I turned to her. She waved for me not to stop. Could she help Perry and Brian? A shudder ran through me as I checked the time, 7:23.

Chapter Twenty-Four

I stomped up the front porch steps. The echo should have brought Brian to the front door of the cabin but didn't. My pulse raced. Was he alive? Where was Perry? Oscar whined and scratched on the door. I turned the doorknob. Oscar burst out and jumped on me licking my face, my hands, whining. I pushed him aside.

"Brian?" I peered into the cabin.

"O?" He mumbled. He pushed a blanket from his lap and tried to stand. I could barely make out his form in the dimly lit room.

I kicked my boots off and rushed to his side. He clasped my hand, and I brushed hair from his face. He moved his legs off the coffee table and winced. My stomach clenched. Perry grunted something from the couch, but my focus was on Brian.

Lilli hesitated at the door. She'd seemed so tough in Franklin, but now she wavered. Oscar turned to sniff Lilli who tensed and jerked back.

"A dog. You didn't say you had a dog." She held out a hand to Oscar who sniffed and wiggled his entire body.

"He likes you." Was she afraid of dogs?

I grabbed Oscar's collar and wrapped my arms around his furry body. He tried to lick my face, and I ducked my face into my shoulder. He wiggled out of my arms and dashed into the yard for zoomies. I chuckled.

Was I actually happy to see this crazy mutt?

Brian tried to stand but fell back into the chair. "You're here. I thought I was dreaming."

Dreams. Was he getting sick?

The fire had died to embers glowing in the hearth. Oscar wiggled past Lilli and into the cabin. Lilli kept her gaze on the dog as she entered the cabin and shut the door. I shrugged out of my coat and reached for the poker. I stirred the embers producing a flame and laid a small piece of wood on it. It caught, and I laid on another, and another.

Lilli set the bag down and shrugged out of her coat. She stared at Oscar who lay sprawled at Brian's feet, then she exhaled. Who was this timid woman, and what was she waiting for? I held up the watch. 9:48. She needed to stabilize Perry and wrap Brian's ankle so we could take the miracle drug to Gracie, right?

Brian lifted his leg back on to the coffee table and moaned. His ankle had swollen to twice its size. We'd gotten back just in time, or hadn't we?

"You did it. I knew you could." He wiped sleep from his eyes.

Had he been talking to Perry? Did Perry think I couldn't do it? Jerk. Lilli rustled through the black bag. "This is Lilli. She's the doctor's assistant."

"Assistant? Perry needs a real doctor." Brian frowned and nodded at Perry on the couch. He hadn't moved since I'd left.

I put a hand on Perry's forehead. "He's burning up."

"Get a rag filled with snow." Lilli set her bag beside the couch. She knelt and pulled back the blanket. Blood had dried on the tattered hole in his jeans, but the bullet wound was swollen and raw. Brian had done the best he could, but I shouldn't have spent the night, no matter how sick I was.

I grabbed a towel from the kitchen and rushed outside. Oscar jumped up and ran onto the porch. He scanned the yard. I filled the towel with snow and handed it to Lilli. She placed it on Perry's forehead.

I slapped my pant leg. "Oscar." He trotted inside.

"He's always on guard now." Brian held his hand out to the dog. Oscar pushed his nose into Brian's hand. "Good boy."

"Wow." I shook my head. "I guess this trip has changed us all."

Brian held my gaze, and my tummy tingled. Was that a glint in his eye? Even now when his ankle throbbed with pain, he could show me how he cared.

I cleared my throat. "What do you need?"

"Do you have water? It seems like this one has mostly slept." She indicated Perry with a nod of her head. "Not that that's a bad thing, but we need to keep these guys hydrated." Lilli unpacked gauze and bottles.

I pulled the tea kettle off the grate in the fireplace and shook it. "This is hot."

"No. We need cold. Melt some snow in it."

I took Perry's glass outside and filled it with snow, brought it inside. Brian held out his glass, and I scooped out half and put it into Brian's cup and poured hot water over both snow-filled cups and handed one to Perry, then to Brian.

"Thanks." Brian sipped the warm water. "Can you help him? I couldn't—"

I frowned. "You're not taking the blame for Perry. Aaron did this to him."

Brian sipped, never taking his gaze from Perry.

Lilly stood, hands on her hips. "You're Perry Brewster? I've heard of you." She frowned at him.

"So, I'm famous?" Perry mumbled.

I held the glass to Perry's lips. He choked but got down a swallow. How did Lilli know him? Had he and Aaron been to Franklin too?

"Do you need more hot water or…" I cleared my throat. "I mean, what can I do?" I kept my eyes on her face. She hadn't moved a muscle since she'd recognized Perry. They had history. So did I, but we had to move beyond that. Didn't she understand?

She sighed. "I will need more hot water, but first, hold his hands while I cleanse and dress that wound." She shook her head. "This won't be pleasant."

"I…" My hand fluttered to my face.

Lilli pulled out a thermometer and ran it across Perry's forehead. The thermometer beeped, and she grunted. "We need to hurry." She glanced at Brian. "You're next."

"I'm not going anywhere." Brian closed his eyes.

I knelt beside the couch and clutched Perry's hands in mine. He was burning up.

****

The fire snapped and popped like a breakfast cereal commercial. I glanced at Grandpa Billy's watch. 11:12. We'd been here over an hour already.

"Scissors." Lilli held out a hand.

I reached into her bag and pulled out scissors, handing them to her by the handle.

She snipped the cloth tape she would use to bind Brian's ankle. "Thanks." Lilli placed the scissors and the roll of tape back in the bag and lifted Brian's heel. He grimaced, and she hesitated. I took Brian's hand.

"You have a knack for healing." She glanced at me. "Do you have training?"

I shook my head. "I always wanted to work with horses for a living, but that all changed when El Primo hit, and then novel hepatitis A virus…" My mouth went dry. Why had I said that?

It was the truth, though. "Everything changed after the storms, but when my family started dying, I didn't know what to do. I lost hope."

I glanced at Lilli who packed her supplies into the pouches and folds of the medical bag. "I can't sit by as my loved ones die. Never again."

Lilli nodded. I stared into the fire, blinking back tears. Brian's regular breathing eased my fears. If he could sleep, the pain meds were working. Perry lay on the couch, silent. The color in his cheeks had turned from angry red to a mild pink, but he seemed to have shrunk. Lilli sat on the edge of the coffee table and waited for me to pull myself together.

I cleared my throat. "I thought I would die, too, each time someone—"

"Don't." Lilli put a hand on my shoulder.

"I did die a little bit, I guess. I don't want to experience that helplessness again."

A strange sense of calm enveloped me. If I could save lives, maybe I could make up for all the death—

Lilli's eyes twinkled, and she shrugged. "We all have a story, and most of them these days come with pain." She ran a hand across her forehead, and the collar of her button-down shirt opened to expose part of a tattoo. I could make out "chicks." She'd left her partner behind to save lives, even Perry's. I wanted to learn everything she knew about healing and forgiveness.

"I better check on Top Hat's lame leg." I moved to the back door in a trance, my head swimming with ideas of helping Lilli and Dr. N.

Top Hat raised his head, his bright eyes staring right into mine. I grinned and opened the stall door. He took a step toward me. "Are you feeling better?" I patted his neck and hooked a lead rope on his halter. I led him out of the stall, but he didn't limp. Did he? Or was it just wishful thinking?

****

The sky had cleared, and snow melted off the roof, drip, drip, drip. The spring thaw had resumed, and a mist hung in the sweet mountain air. I gazed at Mount Rainier in the distance as I stepped off the porch. Slush covered the steps, and Oscar's thawing paw prints crisscrossed the yard.

Brian slipped out the door. Lilli must be checking on Perry. He waited on the porch. Did he want to say something to me? My stomach tingled. Maybe he wanted to kiss me goodbye. I was going to miss him, but we'd send help.

I stared at the sturdy porch beams. "This is a great place."

Brian grunted and shook his head. "This place saved our lives."

My eyes watered, and I wiped at them. This was no time to be sentimental. We had to head back to Cedarville. They'd waited too long for the doctor and the medicine.

"Will you be okay with Perry?" What was I asking him? Did he have a choice? His ankle was sprained, not broken, but he couldn't make the journey back to Cedarville with us, not without a great deal of pain.

"We'll send a rescue team for you."

He glanced at his hands. "I'll be fine, but don't take too long, okay?"

Was he nervous? I was. I nodded and rocked onto my heels. Grandpa Billy's watch hung like a weight around my wrist. I read the time. 11:38. I slipped it off my wrist and held it out to him.

Our fingers touched, and the electric pulse of that contact ran a shiver through my body. He held it in his palm and caressed the watch face. He stood mute, then cocked his head and gazed at me with his eyes dark. "What are you doing? I can't take this."

"You'll need it to keep track of time." I couldn't hold his gaze, and my throat constricted. I glanced at the watch. "Keep it safe for me until I see you again." I wiped my eyes with my sleeve and followed him into the cabin.

Why hadn't he kissed me? Did I expect him to? Was that why I gave it to him?

Was I disappointed? No. His whole body was bruised, and he was as lame as Top Hat. They'd both be staying here. Kissing was the last thing on his mind. Besides, we'd see each other again.

Perry's chest rose and fell in a regular pattern, and Lilli had cleaned his face. He slept, which was what he needed right now. Lilli crouched over her bag, trying to control her smile. She reloaded her equipment and supplies for our trek to Samson's. If she said anything about me and Brian…

What would I do, punch her in the shoulder? No. I was embarrassed. I wanted to keep my emotions about Brian to myself until I understood them. She glanced at my naked wrist and nodded. Did she know how

important that watch was to me? I glanced at her, but her smile was gone. I grabbed my coat.

I glanced at Brian who caressed the watch face with his thumb.

I cleared my throat. "I guess I'll pack up my stuff." I reached for the sweater I'd draped over the back of the chair, and scanned the cabin. What was I saying? I didn't have anything to pack. Lilli bent over Perry's wound, wrapping it as he groaned. I opened the door to the carport and escaped the claustrophobic cabin.

Oscar nudged my leg, trying to squeeze past me and out the doorway. "Oh no you don't." I knelt to grab his collar. "You're staying with Brian."

Oscar tilted his head, a toothy grin on his scruffy face. I chuckled and pushed him into the cabin, easing the door shut. Top Hat's ears perked up, and he gazed at me. His mouth dripped strands of hay. Did he know I was leaving? He knew something was up.

"We'll send the rescue team for you too." I threw another armful of hay into the stall, and he nudged my shoulder. "I'm sorry."

He snorted in my face. "Really?" I ran my hand under his mane, the hair smooth and warm. I inhaled the musky odor of clean hay and horse dander. He was beautiful, and I hated to leave him.

"At least it's downhill all the way, right?"

I jumped. Lilli stood on the step, leaning on the closed door. Was she finished with Perry? Apparently. That meant—

She put a hand on my shoulder. "He'll be fine. The sooner we leave, the sooner we can send help. Besides, Jade and Dr. Nordby are following us, remember? Dr. N will check my work."

Right. Like Franklin was going to let Dr. N leave. They needed her too, right?

I shrugged. "I know. It's hard for me to leave Brian and Top Hat here." Did I say that out loud? My vision blurred.

She frowned and nodded. "I'll be ready in five."

How had she left Jade and all those kids, her kids? She understood me better than I did. She closed the door, and I was alone with Top Hat. I picked up a brush and ran it over his back. He grunted, and I groomed him with automatic motions.

At least the snow was melting. It would be easier for a rescue team to transport Perry and Brian. Besides, Dr. N would be here soon with Jade. That's the only thing that kept Lilli moving toward Cedarville, the fact that Jade and their beautiful children would join her there.

Lilli was right. It was downhill all the way.

I ran the brush through Top Hat's tail. He seemed so different now, like he could read my mind. We'd become a team. I caressed his neck. Top Hat sniffed my jacket. Why had Mr. G only used him for trail rides? He could have been a show horse, a blue-ribbon winner. He bumped my cheek with his huge nose.

"You were too smart to go in round in circles in that stupid, old arena, weren't you?" I blew into his nostril, and he huffed back at me. He needed a job, a purpose, just like I did. "We're going to save lives, aren't we?" I ran a hand down his face, then patted him on the neck. Picked up my pack, then walked to the front porch.

Brian waved from the window, and I gazed at him, a muscle in my neck tightening. What if Aaron returned? Brian had the gun, but Aaron was desperate. My head buzzed, and my legs wobbled. I took a deep breath and focused on the edge of the bluff.

Lilli emerged from the cabin, a string of orders spewing from her lips. "It's noon now, so we'll head straight to Cedar Hills Farm."

I nodded. "Gracie was so sick when we left."

"I hope we're in time. Then Brian told me about Mary's grandparents, so we'll make a quick stop there, then to Silver Springs Stable, and finally Cedarville and the clinic." She glanced at me. "It's almost ten o'clock. Let's hit the road."

I nodded and slipped my pack on, tightening the straps. Lilli fell in step beside me.

I snuck another glance at the window that framed Brian's face. The bags under his eyes were dark purple, and my stomach bunched into a knot. I raised my hand in a final salute.

Chapter Twenty-Five

I slid and skidded on the melting snow at the side of the road as we circumnavigated another pile of windblown trees. I still found myself checking for cars that hadn't traveled these roads for over a year. The landscape turned greener the closer we got to Cedar Hills Farm, with trees covered in blossoms standing in the distance like cotton balls of white and pink. We traveled in silence.

I stopped and scanned the landscape. Did something move? I peered down the road, but there were so many places for a person to hide in the bushes or behind a tree. As long as it wasn't Aaron. Why did I leave the gun with Brian?

Because I was never going to shoot anyone, that's why.

Someone stepped out of the underbrush and stood in the middle of the road, and my heart skipped a beat. It was Aaron. I froze.

"You killed my brother." Aaron waved a long stick with a pointed end. He jabbed it at me, and I stumbled backward.

Had he lost his mind? His eyes were red rimmed, as though he'd been crying or hadn't slept, or both. His clothes hung in filthy rags, wet from the mist or maybe a fall in the creek. He waved the stick again, and I backed into a tree.

"Perry's alive. He's at the cabin." Lilli's voice rang out loud and confident.

"Liar." Aaron paced the road. "He's dead. I saw him. She made me shoot him." He jabbed the spear at me again, then glaring at me, he ran his hand through his long, tangled hair.

"You're just saying that so I'll let you pass, but I'm not stupid. You made me shoot him, and you're not getting away with it."

"She's telling the truth, Aaron." I pressed my back into the tree, ready to run behind it and into the woods if I had to. My voice shook as I tried again to calm him. "He's alive and waiting for you." I held my body still, my face blank. I couldn't show fear, but it exuded from every pore.

Aaron glared at me. "Shut up."

Lilli took a step forward. "I cleaned and treated his wound, and he's recovering in the cabin. He was asking about you, wanted to know if you were okay."

I had to warn her about Aaron. "Lilli."

She spun around, her eyes pinpricks in her face. "He's just a kid."

I gasped. Her words hit me like a punch in the gut. She turned back to Aaron and pointed up the mountain.

"You should go tell him yourself." She didn't mention that it was uphill all the way.

Aaron's shoulders slumped and shook, and he dropped to his knees.

Was he crying?

I tensed. Lilli walked to Aaron with slow, even steps. Would Aaron hurt her? She rummaged in her bag and pulled out a purple water bottle, then held it out to him. I stared at the bottle, then at Lilli. She ignored me.

"You need water." She took a step closer.

"Why would you help me?" he replied, his voice thick with emotion.

"We must help each other, or we'll never survive." Lilli stepped closer, and Aaron grimaced, but he took the bottle. She turned and walked to me. Aaron took a step after her, then another. I tensed, but the closer he got, the smaller he seemed.

I turned my eyes away, unable to meet Lilli's. She was generous with someone I would have left at the side of the road. He was skin and bones. Why hadn't I noticed that before? Lilli was right, we needed to help one another, or we'd turn into monsters.

Lilli adjusted her pack on her shoulders. "You can keep my water bottle. I'll share with Olivia."

"You will?" I frowned at her. "I mean, of course."

I had hated Aaron for so long, even while Perry and I had dated. Could I change my mind about him now?

Lilli's behavior made no sense to me, but he'd responded to her without yelling or threatening her. Then it hit me. She'd given Aaron respect, had eye contact, gave him a smile to calm him. Would I ever be that strong?

Lilli pulled a muffin from her bag and handed it to him. He nodded, then turned and walked away. He stuffed half the muffin in his mouth as he headed into the mountains to find his brother. He didn't glance back.

That part I understood, but I was still grappling with Lilli's lack of fear. He was Perry's little brother, right? The other half of the "Brewster boys."

Lilli turned and, with one final glance over her shoulder, walked in the opposite direction. "They have food at the cabin, right? He'll need a good meal."

I nodded and followed in silence. Aaron would have hurt me if Lilli hadn't intervened, but would he have, really? How could something as simple as the offering of water change his mind? I shook my head. Respect was as powerful as any drug. I sighed. But what about our attitude toward each other? Sure, we all needed water, but we also needed someone who cared.

****

I daydreamed of my warm soft bed in my cozy room at home as we trudged downhill. Lilli stopped, and I yawned and stretched. The road disappeared around a bend, the trees blocking our view.

She stood with her hands on her hips. "I just have to know. Are we getting close?"

I rubbed my eyes and shook my head. She was exhausted, and so was I. "I remember that bend in the road. That's where Brian lost Old Charlie, so probably another fifteen or twenty minutes." I pulled out my water bottle and took a swig. She didn't need to hear about Aaron and Perry's ambush. That was history.

Lilli stared at something in the sky. I gazed into the bright blue expanse. Condors, two of them, circling so high they looked like black dots. Were they waiting for something to die or just waiting their turn to feast on the corpse?

"We need to make a plan. I mean once we get to Samson's."

"Okay." I wiped my nose and stared at the road. Shouldn't she be telling me what to do? I shrugged. "You're going to prepare a concoction for Gracie?" I stopped, but she didn't respond. "And I'm going to help you?"

"Okay. I'll leave a vial of tonic with Barb and instructions on preparation and dosage, then we head to Cedarville today and set up the clinic. Dr. Johnson has waited long enough for help. We need to begin treating people right away."

"Wait. Do you mean we aren't going to treat Gracie? And what about our stop at Mary's grandma's or Mr. G's?" I shifted my weight from one foot to the other.

"Treating Gracie and making stops will take too long. We need to go straight to Cedarville. Samson could bring his kids in to town. The faster we get set up, the more people we can—"

"No. It won't. That was the original plan I had with Dr. N." I clenched my fists. "Brian and I promised we'd bring help." I glared at her. "We have to save Gracie."

Lilli scratched her head. Why was she changing her mind? Because she wasn't a real doctor? Dr. N would stop and help Gracie, right? I glared at her.

She sighed. "Fine, but we need to reach Cedarville by nightfall."

****

Lilli and I plodded downhill in a light rain. The descent pulled us along, and we made good time, but I was drenched to the skin and miserable. She must be too. I glanced over my shoulder, and Lilli was right there, her frown punctuated by thin pressed lips. She was on a mission.

A breeze blew through the treetops, and they swayed. I wiped rain from my eyelashes.

"Why did you stop?" Lilli gazed down Highway 96 to another bend in the road.

"Shhh." I tensed. "Something is coming. Hear it?"

Dogs barked in the distance, mixed with the sound

of men talking.

"Dogs." Lilli crouched.

Was she preparing to jump into the underbrush?

I gulped. "Hunters?"

"Dogs. A whole pack." Lilli glanced from me to the bend in the road ahead.

A man walked around the corner talking with another, but he stopped when he caught sight of us. He held up a hand, and the other man stopped. Two more men walked up beside him, four in all.

"Oh, my goddess. Now what?" Lilli put a hand to her throat.

Did she just say "goddess"? I stared at her. "Do you know Emma?"

"What? More pressing issues right now, Olivia."

"Right." I focused on the men. They stood in the road, blocking our view. The one holding up his hand called to us.

"We are looking for two teens. Have you seen anyone up here?" The man took a couple steps and stopped.

I squinted at him. "Dr. Woolf?" Rain fell in a drizzle, and the light breeze blew it in my face, blurring my vision. "It's me, Olivia." I took a step forward.

"Olivia?" Dr. Woolf pulled off his hat. "Thank the stars. Are you okay?" He peered behind me. "Is that Brian with you?"

"No, but Brian's okay. He sprained his ankle and is waiting in a cabin for Dr. Nordby. We left him about an hour and a half from here." I walked to him. He took my hand and pulled me into a hug. He caught me off guard, but I was too exhausted to resist.

"The doctor had an emergency as we were preparing

to leave. She said she'd follow soon." Lilli's voice startled me.

"Oh yeah." I turned. "This is Lilli."

"Lilith Christine DeVries. Pleased to meet you." Lilli held out her hand to Dr. Woolf.

I motioned to Lillie. "This is Dr. Nordby's assistant," then to Dr. Woolf, "and this is Dr. Woolf from Cedarville."

"I've heard of you." Dr. Woolf clasped her hand and shook. He gave me the side-eye. "Thank heavens we found you in one piece. Mrs. Z is ready to skin Mr. G and Samson alive." He chuckled. Was it from relief?

Josh joined our circle and smiled at Lilli. "So, your name is Lilli? You're not Emma's Lilli, are you?"

Lilli stood on her toes and scanned the group behind Josh. "Emma? Is she here?"

"Emma's Lilli?" Dr. Woolf shook his head.

I shook my head and turned away. Emma's Lilli?

"Where's Jade?" Josh scanned the road behind us.

"How do you know Lilli?" Dr. Woolf frowned at his son.

"Wait, you mean this is Emma's Lilli?" I shook my head. "Emma told us all about you and Jade. You saved her life." I glanced from Lilli to Josh. "I've been traveling with bless-all-the-goddesses Lilli all this time?"

Lilli held her hand out to Josh. "Lilith Christine DeVries at your service." She made a bow.

****

The rain dripped off branches, and the sun shone, warming the April air. I'd been gone for three days, but it seemed like weeks. I stretched my aching shoulders and back as we hiked down the asphalt road but meeting the rescue party had lifted my heavy heart, and finding out Lilli was Emma's friend made her seem more like an old friend.

"That was kind of weird, meeting that search party." Lilli clutched her medical bag as she walked.

"I can't believe you're Emma's Lilli." I turned to face her. "I mean, I was hoping the rescue team would show up, but when Josh figured out you were Emma's Lilli? That was cool." I sighed. "Emma's going to freak."

"It's a miracle she's alive. We didn't know if she'd make it to Cedarville when we left her. She didn't know north from south back then."

"Josh found her. They're together now."

"Emma and Josh? Is he a good guy?"

I glanced at her. Was she being protective of Emma? "Yes. He is a good guy. He's part of the rescue team, isn't he?"

She nodded and kicked a stone from the road.

"We take care of each other, especially since—"

I blinked. Since what? Since most of the town had died. Lilli placed a hand on my shoulder. I wiped my eyes. Bless-all-the-goddesses Lilli and I hiked side by side, our shoulders touching.

Chapter Twenty-Six

Oscar barked and ran to the door, sniffing. Brian stood and glanced out the window. Now what? It was like Grand Central Station around here. He hobbled to the door.

"Are you expecting anyone?" Brian glanced at Perry.

Brian lifted the curtain. How long before the doctor arrived? Perry stirred on the couch, and Brian dragged his sore ankle as he moved toward him. He kicked Oscar who yelped.

"Sorry, Oscar." Brian bent down to rub his ankle. Oscar pushed his nose into Brian's hand. He needed forgiveness, even if it was from the dog.

Perry opened his eyes. He yawned.

Brian placed a hand on Perry's forehead. "How are you feeling?"

Perry nodded but didn't speak. He closed his eyes again. Brian held a glass of water to Perry's lips until he drank.

"Any sign of the doctor?" Perry pulled the blanket up to his chin.

"No." Brian leaned on the chairs to hobble to the window. He pulled back the curtain for the millionth time and jerked back. He rubbed his eyes, then stared down the driveway. Two women and a tangle of kids trudged through the snow straight toward the cabin. "Yes. Someone is here."

"Friend or foe?" Perry chuckled.

Brian cocked his eyebrow at Perry. He must be feeling better if he could crack a lame joke.

Two women and seven children congregated on the porch. He limped to the door and yanked it open.

"Hello." The older woman took off a glove and held out a hand. "I'm Doctor Alicia Nordby. You must be Brian." She smiled.

Brian took her hand. "We've been expecting you." He glanced over the doctor's shoulder.

"This is Jade, and I'll let her introduce her children." She motioned to all the kids. He counted six plus the baby in her arms. Seven kids?

He opened the door wider and stood back. "Come in. I am Brian, and this is Perry. He's been shot."

The doctor entered the house and knelt by Perry's side. She pulled back the blanket. "Hmm."

What did that mean? Brian leaned against the chair by the fireplace as she opened her medical kit. Jade ushered the kids into the cabin, holding the baby in her arms. They swarmed around the fireplace, crowding Oscar into a corner.

How could she have seven kids? Probably the same way Mrs. Z had two teenagers. Jade laid the baby on a chair cushion and squatted by the chair, then helped each child take off coats, scarves, and boots. Two older children did those things for themselves. *Seven kids?*

"Any water? Lilli did a fine job, but I want to inspect the wound. I'll need to wash and disinfect it again."

"Sure." Brian shuffled to the fireplace and poured some hot water in a bowl.

Dr. Nordby placed a hand on Perry's shoulder. "Let's have a look, shall we?" She took the end of the bandage and began unwrapping.

Brian sighed with relief. The swollen wound made him cringe, but she didn't seem concerned. He glared at Perry. Why couldn't he hate this guy? Olivia never even glanced at him when she was with Perry. But now? They had been stuck in this cabin together. He was annoyed, but angry? Nah.

He shook his head. It didn't matter anymore. He just wanted Perry to live so they could go home. He glanced at Jade and the kids.

She shrugged. "I didn't birth a one of them, but they are mine now, if that makes sense." Her steely gaze hit him like a slap, and he stepped back.

He nodded. Don't rile the mother bear. She arranged the kids near the flames as Dr. Nordby worked on Perry.

Dr. Nordby pulled out a hypodermic needle, filled it with a golden liquid, and injected it into Perry's arm. "That should do it. He'll sleep now, which is the best medicine."

"You. Sit." She smiled at Brian and patted the chair.

He'd spent every minute since Olivia left in that stupid thing, but he dropped into it. Anything to get home.

"Let's examine that ankle." She pulled the bag to the chair and knelt beside him.

"What's wrong with the man?" one of Jade's boys asked.

"He fell off a cliff—" Jade began but didn't get to finish.

"A cliff? And he ain't dead yet?" The boy stared at him with huge brown eyes. His tiny face was a healthy pink from their trek from Franklin.

Perry scoffed, and Brian shot him a scowl. How would they feed all these kids? They must be starving after their walk down the mountain. There might be enough canned soup—

Dr. Nordby lifted his ankle, and he winced. It had ballooned to two and a half times its normal size, but he hadn't taken his shoe off. Could she do anything at this stage?

She untied the boot laces and pulled it off. He hissed air through his clenched teeth. With gentle hands, she moved his foot from side to side and flexed and pointed it. He tensed, but she didn't push the limits of his pain. He sighed and relaxed into the chair.

"It's not broken. That's a relief." She reached into her bag for rubbing alcohol, poured some in her hands, and rubbed it over the ankle. She pulled out a bandage roll and began to wrap it.

"Ow." He tensed his body and gritted his teeth, gripping the chair arms.

She glanced at him but didn't stop. He closed his eyes. She worked with quick precision and placed his foot on the coffee table. Brian exhaled as he rubbed his hand down his leg. His ankle throbbed.

"RICE." She stood with her hands on her hips.

"Rest. Ice. Compress. Elevate." Brian glanced at the watch. 1:16.

"Yep." She reached into her bag, pulling out a bottle. "A few pain pills won't hurt either." She shook out two and handed them to him.

"So, when can I walk? We need to get back to Cedarville." He took the glass she handed him.

"Walk? You won't be walking without pain for

weeks. This cabin is perfect. You can rest and heal for a couple more days." She focused on packing her bag.

Days? He slumped into the chair.

Jade sang "You Are My Sunshine" as the kids warmed by the fire, and Brian's eyelids began to close. What had she given him? He needed to catch up with Olivia, but all he wanted…to…do…was—

****

Cedar Hills shone from the roof of Samson's barn. The air hung in eerie silence with the occasional birdsong as I searched the pastures for children at play. Lilli increased her pace, and I jogged to keep up. I glanced at my wrist. Brian had the watch. He'd be fine, right?

Lilli stopped, and I collided with her.

"This Samson's place?"

"Yes."

She pressed her lips into a thin line, then spoke. "You know the plan. In and out. Administer medicine, sterilize as we go, then back on the road."

I nodded. My nerves bunched in the eerie quiet. Had Gracie died? Was that the cloud hanging over the farm? Barb appeared on the porch, and I waved from the driveway. Her blonde hair stood on her head in a disheveled knot. She wore a terry cloth robe tied tight around her small waist. She held up a hand to stop us.

"The kids are sick, even Samson," she called.

"I brought help." I took a step forward, dragging Lilli with me.

Lilli waved. Barb shielded her eyes and frowned. Didn't she believe me?

"Hand me my bag." Lilli held up the black case. "I have medicine."

208

Barb wiped tears from her cheeks. "Olivia? I hardly recognized you."

I put a hand to my face. I was exhausted, but adrenaline pumped through my veins. Was that all that kept me going? Lilli and I approached Barb. She stood her ground. I reached out a hand as I climbed the steps.

"Dr. N sent me. She's coming as soon as she can." Lilli joined me on the porch. "I'm Lilli, her assistant."

"What?" Barb gave a sob. "The doctor is finally coming?" Barb took Lilli by the arm, and they disappeared into the house. I followed. The air was stale with hints of rotten egg, but it didn't stink like death.

Yet.

I made my way on tiptoes to the bedroom at the end of the hall. Gracie lay on the bed, her cheeks red, her body still. Lilli ran a thermometer across her forehead. I stood at the door, and Barb stood at the foot of the bed, her arms crossed.

Lilli pulled out a thermometer. "I'm going to miss these when the batteries finally wear out." She ran it across Gracie's forehead until it beeped. She glanced at it. "101.3. Not too high."

She reached into the bag and pulled out a vial, gave it a gentle shake, and pulled out a hypodermic needle. I turned my eyes away. I'd have to work on that if I wanted to help people.

Lilli administered the shot in one breath and applied a bandage. "Who's next?" Lilli stood, ready for her next patient.

"Our boys." Barb led her down the hall to another bedroom. "This is the sickroom." She opened the door.

Three single beds were arranged around the room, each one covered with a tangle of colorful quilts and blankets, small arms and legs protruding from the piles. They must be feverish and restless under the covers.

Barb stopped beside the bed closest to the door. "You can start with Mark."

"Where's Mary?" I asked.

"She's with her aunt in Cedarville. They're expecting you in town." She put her fingers to her lips. "I can't believe—"

I placed a hand on her shoulder, and she squeezed my fingers. "I told you I'd bring help."

"You couldn't have come at a better time." Barb's cheeks shone with her tears.

"First things first." Lilli bent over a bed and opened the bag.

I leaned against the doorframe as Lilli took Mark's temperature. Barb took the thermometer and placed it in the bag, then pulled out the vial. They worked as a team, like they'd done this every day for months. Barb's face softened as she helped Lilli. I wandered out of the room and down the hallway. Was everyone sick? Maybe Lilli was right. This was taking too long. We still had to get to Mary's grandparents', Mr. G's, then Cedarville.

Chapter Twenty-Seven

I handed a piece of cotton to Lilli, and she wet it with alcohol, wiped the inoculation site on Ben's tiny arm, then applied tape over a piece of cotton. Barb hovered at the door. Her breakdown when Ben whimpered was enough for Lilli to kick her out and for me to take over.

"You'll feel better in no time." Lilli helped him to lie back, pulling the covers up to his neck. Her manners and movements came without effort. I wanted that self-assurance, that ability to calm people and ease their fears. I wanted to heal people, not stand by as they wasted away.

Barb's eyes twinkled as she gazed upon her son, and her love for him warmed me to my core. I looked away. I cleared my throat and focused on Lilli as I handed her vials and packets of gauze that she repacked in her bag. This type of work was more than satisfying. It meant Barb and Samson could continue their lives together. Their kids could grow up and grow old. I sighed. Helping them helped me.

"They'll be fine in a couple days." Lilli smiled at Barb and led her from the room with a light touch to her elbow. "Their symptoms may seem to worsen, and they may be a bit lethargic, but that should pass by tomorrow. If not, send word to the Cedarville Clinic ASAP."

"Thank you, thank you." Barb pulled me into a hug.

"Samson said you'd come through for us, and he was right. You did. You're just like your dad." She smiled at me. "He always kept his word. We miss him so much."

My eyes blurred for a moment, but I swallowed and nodded. "I'm just glad we got here when we did." I caught Lilli's grin as she turned and carried her black bag outside.

This whole process, arrival, administration of shots, soothing the kids, filled me with a need to hurry mixed with calm, like it was scary important, and I was always meant to do it. I lifted my wrist but couldn't check the time. Even with Lilli's speed in checking each patient and her precise answers to Barb keeping us on our tight schedule, my shoulders tensed.

Would we be in time to save Mary's grandmother, though? I pushed that emotion down. We had two more stops to make before Cedarville, and Mary's grandmother was next.

****

The large gate of Mary's grandparents' driveway appeared around a bend, and I glanced at the sky. We'd be lucky to get to Cedarville before dark.

"It looks deserted." Lilli marched to the front porch. "You stay here, and I'll run in and take a look."

I stood at the foot of the steps. "Anyone home?"

Lilli opened the door and walked in. I frowned. What did she think—

Lilli poked her head out the door and waved me into the house. "She's in here."

I rushed up the stairs and into the house. Mary's grandmother lay sprawled on the floor, her skin a pasty white. A cloying aroma permeated the walls. I put a hand to my nose and glanced at Lilli.

"Help me get her on the couch, then bring some water. I'll check upstairs."

I nodded and grabbed her feet, while Lilli raised her head and shoulders. We hobbled to the couch and laid her in the cushions. I grabbed a blanket from a chair by the fireplace.

"She hasn't been out for long. Look." I pointed to the embers glowing in the fireplace.

Lilli nodded, all business. "Water, quick. I'll be right back." She took the stairs two at a time.

I rushed to the kitchen and tried the faucet. Water gushed out. How did they still have running water? I filled a glass and took it to her. She sipped, then pushed my hands away.

"I'm fine." She coughed and blinked her eyes. Then she closed them. "Bill's upstairs."

"The doctor's assistant is with him now." I sank back on my heels and scanned the room. I took the poker from the hearth and stirred the embers and placed some small pieces of wood on them. The fire was blazing when Lilli clomped down the stairs.

She motioned to me, and I joined her in the kitchen.

"Her husband's body is still warm, so he probably died within the hour." She sighed. "We were too slow." Her shoulders slumped, and she glanced at the woman on the couch, keeping her voice low. "Poor woman worked herself almost to death."

"She doesn't know." My voice wobbled, and I rubbed the back of my neck. "How do we tell her?"

"I'll do it."

I bowed my head. Was this also part of what I wanted to do? I pressed my fingers to my temples, my mind swirling with images of Mom, Dad, Grandpa Billy.

A shiver ran down my spine. If I wanted to help people, now was the time to start.

"You can do this."

I pushed my shoulders back and followed Lilli to the couch. She pulled out the thermometer and ran it across the woman's forehead.

"Does she have a fever?"

"Low-grade. I'll give her some aspirin, and we'll hydrate her." Lilli led me back to the kitchen. "When the rescue team gets back, they'll have to remove the body. In the meantime, let's heat some water so I can clean her up a bit."

I filled the kettle with water, then carried it to the grate in the fireplace. A twinge of regret ran through me. Why hadn't I trusted Lilli from the beginning? She was more than qualified to stand in for Dr. N. She had always deserved it and my respect. I glanced at her.

Lilli took the old lady's pulse with sure, steady movements. "I'm Lilli, and this is Olivia. I have something that will make you feel better."

Mary's grandmother tried to sit but collapsed into the pillow on the couch. "My name is Madrona, but folks call me Maddie." She coughed, and her hand shook as Lilli set it in her lap. "Is Bill—"

Lilli glanced at me, then back to Maddie and nodded. Maddie put a hand to her face, and her shoulders shook, but no sound came from her.

I clenched my teeth and prodded the flames. We hadn't made it in time for Bill. Time. I stared at my empty wrist. I couldn't shake the sense that we would always be late, that the rescue team hadn't made it to the cabin yet, that Dr. N hadn't been able to leave Franklin. My shoulders ached.

****

Lilli put a hand on Maddie's shoulder. "No going up or down stairs. The rescue team will be here later today."

"But Bill—" Maddie put a hand to her chest.

"Mary will need her grandma, so you need to do as I say and recover for her." Lilli nodded and placed a tall glass of water on the table by the couch for her.

Maddie pulled the blanket under her chin, and soon her breathing had grown regular and sonorous. Lilli stood and grabbed her bag.

My chest constricted. We had to leave her with her dead husband upstairs. She'd survive until someone could bring her to the hospital, but to leave her alone with her grief seemed cruel.

We tromped out the door and walked shoulder to shoulder across Maddie and Bill's back pasture to the trail that would lead us to Mr. G's. The cloying scent of illness and death lingered in the air. I couldn't speak.

I led us down an old cow trail into the woods and to the back gate. My muscles ached from our trek, but I clamped my mouth shut. Complaining wouldn't get us to Mr. G's any faster.

****

I wiped my brow with my hoodie sleeve and glanced at Lilli who huffed and puffed beside me. Why did this have to be uphill? At least Lilli hadn't asked if we were there yet. She had a sense of humor that one, and skills at healing. It made this trip bearable.

I peered through the trees. We had to be getting close. I stopped in the middle of the trail.

Was that the red of Mr. G's barn? It sat like a beacon in the distance, and my chest filled with warmth.

Lilli bumped into me, then leaned against my

shoulder. "Are we—"

"Yep."

"Bless all the goddesses." She smiled, and we hiked to the gate that I'd opened for Brian four days ago. What would Mr. G say when I told him about Top Hat? I sighed. Would Old Charlie be there?

I closed the gate behind us, and we marched over the top of the hill and out of the trees. Mr. G walked out of the barn and onto the driveway, and Old Charlie trumpeted his greeting. He had made it.

I stopped and took in the scene. Old Charlie's golden coat gleamed in the sun, and Mr. G waved. I waved and began to run down the hill. I couldn't stop smiling, and my cheeks ached with the unfamiliar exercise.

Mr. G held his hat in his hands as he made his way to us.

"You're alive." He had yet to smile, but his eyes shone bright. "When Old Charlie turned up without you, well…" He shrugged. "I didn't know…" His voice caught. "I figured the Brewsters had gotten Top Hat and that—" He scanned the hill behind us. "Did they?"

"I wouldn't ever let that happen." I put a hand on his shoulder. "He pulled up lame, and we left him behind with Brian to rest a bit more, but he's fine other than that."

"Oh." He wiped his forehead with his kerchief and let loose a stream of questions. "Was it a front leg or a hind? Did you wrap it? Where is Brian? Are you okay?" He glanced past me to Lilli.

"Brian sprained his ankle, so he stayed behind with Top Hat. They're both lame." Did I mean lame as in dork? No. I shrugged. "But I brought help. This is Lill—

"

"Lilith Christine DeVries." She held out her hand, and he clasped it.

"I'm pleased to meet you. Thanks for getting her back in one piece."

"She brought me." Lilli bobbed her chin at me.

Mr. G nodded. "That I believe. I'm just glad she's okay, and that boy of hers too." He frowned at me. "You could do a lot worse, you know?"

I stared at him and stuttered. "Wha—" What did he mean, I could do a lot worse? Lilli chuckled, and heat rose from my chest to my cheeks. I guess I'd better get used to people commenting on Brian. I'd done that to myself, right? Maybe he'd never really been a dork.

Mr. G held up a hand and swatted the air. "You don't have to think about that yet. You're too young. The important thing is you're back with the medicine." He gave Lilli a nod. "You're probably in a hurry to get to Cedarville. Am I right?"

Lilli nodded, and I wobbled. Mr. G reached out a hand to steady me.

"Hey, missy. You're not one hundred percent yet." Lilli grabbed my other arm before I could topple.

"If it weren't for the snowstorm, and Brian falling off a cliff, and me getting sick, we'd have been back that same day, and you wouldn't have had to worry." I had to pull myself together. We were almost home.

"Never you mind about that." Mr. G helped me sit on an overturned bucket.

Lilli released my arm and put her hands on her hips. "This girl is a hero, you know?"

"I do know." He gave me a wink. "You did it. You got hay for my horses, and you brought medicine for the

217

town. You are a hero." Mr. G pushed his thin hair from his eyes.

"Brian is too." Heat rose to my face yet again. I needed to change the subject, now. "How's Angel?"

"She has a healthy filly at her side." He shook his head. "It was touch and go."

"Nice." I stared at the gravel in front of the bucket. "Mabel would be so happy."

"She's smiling down, I know it." He stared at the mountain, and I sighed. Mount Rainier was a silent constant in our lives, while we changed with every second, every illness, every death, every victory. We changed whether we wanted to or not.

Lilli put a hand on my forehead and took my pulse. "She'll need water before we go."

"Right." Mr. G crossed the driveway in large strides and entered the house. He returned with two glasses of water. Mr. G motioned with his head, and he and Lilli walked to the lawn. I took in Mount Rainier standing in the distance. Lilli mumbled something I couldn't make out. Were they worried about something?

Lilli cleared her throat. "It's time. We need to head out."

Mr. G pulled a watch with a broken band from his pocket. "It's 2:47." He fit his hat on his head. "I'll drive you as far as the logjam. It's only a half mile to Cedarville from there." Mr. G smiled at me. "It's the least I can do for the kid who saved my horses and found the doc. I'll get my keys." He disappeared into the house.

"He called me a doc." Lilli beamed.

I chuckled and held out a hand. She pulled me to my feet and into a hug. I was almost home with the medicine and with Lilli. Mr. G skidded the truck to a halt, and we climbed in beside him.

Chapter Twenty-Eight

Oscar jumped to his feet and growled. He ran to the door and whined. Brian shook off the sleep and roused himself to stand. He hobbled to the door. "What is it now?" He ran his hand over Oscar's head as he pulled back the curtain.

Brian jerked back and let the curtain fall, then lifted it again. "What is he doing here?" He scanned the table.

Jade held a sleeping baby. "Who's here?" She put a finger to her lips to shush the kids sitting at the table. The other three were checking out books against the back wall, oblivious to danger. He glanced out the window. Dr. N stood at the kitchen counter. She glanced over her shoulder but kept on packing her medical bag.

Aaron paced in the driveway in front of the cabin. He cupped his hands and called, "Perry," in a plaintive voice. He shuffled his feet but didn't approach.

Brian scratched his head and gripped Oscar's collar. Oscar wanted out, so maybe he should go out. He'd protect the kids and Jade. Brian turned the doorknob, and Oscar's head tilted. The dog gave him eye contact, wagging his whole body. "Sit."

"What's up?" Perry raised his upper body resting on his elbows.

Brian frowned at Perry. "Aaron is here. Is he going to behave?"

"Aaron? Oh my God. Aaron, no." Perry sat and winced. "Help me to the window. He won't stop until he sees me."

"Whoa. Why is my patient moving?" Dr. N crossed the room and placed a hand on Perry's shoulder.

"Who is Aaron?" Dr. N pushed down on Perry's shoulder.

"You don't understand. He. Needs. Me." Perry swatted her hand away. "Just do it." Perry glared at Brian.

Brian nodded at Dr. N who took Perry's arm while Brian took the other, and with a cry, Perry stood.

"Perry?" Aaron paced in the driveway. "You in there?"

Brian teetered, off-balance by Perry's weight. "Great. Say something, or he's going to charge."

"I'm all right, Aaron. I'm okay."

"You know the rules. I need to see you."

Six kids stood staring out the windows with open mouths. Brian glanced at Jade, and she nodded consent.

"No way." Brian shook his head. It was bad enough being stuck in here with Perry, but both the Brewsters with all these kids and two women? "No."

"You have to let him in. He's sopping wet. He can't stay out in the cold." Jade's jaw clenched as she glared at him.

Brian glanced from Jade to Dr. N, to Perry, then to Aaron shivering outside. It was as if Aaron linked heart and soul to Perry. Brian sighed and cracked the door. Oscar lunged, but Brian gritted his teeth and grabbed the dog with one hand. "Not. Yet. Dog."

Dr. N shifted Perry's weight. He was going to crush her if they didn't do something quick.

"Perry?" Aaron took a step toward the cabin but kept a wary eye on Oscar.

The dog didn't bark but kept Aaron in his sight. Perry clung to Dr. N, but Brian couldn't hold Oscar much longer. If he let the dog loose, he might attack.

"Get in here," Brian called and waved Aaron into the cabin. "Hurry, before we lose all our heat." Brian wrestled Oscar to the side as Aaron rushed into the cabin to Perry's side. Brian eased the door closed but kept hold of Oscar's collar. Oscar sniffed after Aaron but didn't growl.

"Perry." He hugged his brother, and Dr. N took a step back. Aaron helped Perry back to the couch. He sat beside him and held his hand. "I swear I didn't mean to shoot you, bro."

Sweat beaded on Perry's forehead. Brian cringed at the pain written on Perry's face. He'd endured the pain of appearing at the window for his younger brother's sake. Aaron's mouth worked, but no words came out.

"Shut up, Aaron." Perry punched Aaron's shoulder. "You've been wanting to shoot me for sixteen years."

Aaron sobbed and buried his head against Perry's shirt. Perry smirked at Brian.

"Now you're really going to need the pain meds." Dr. N frowned.

Aaron jumped off the couch, glaring at Dr. N.

"Sit down, bro. They're helping me."

"Brothers." Brian shrugged. He released Oscar, who had lost interest in Aaron and curled up in front of the fire.

"That could have gone worse." Brian shrugged at Dr. N and hobbled to the kitchen. "I'll put some soup on."

Brian glanced out the window over the kitchen sink. Top Hat circled in his stall with a decided limp. Brian turned to glance at Aaron. No one had cleaned the stall since Olivia left for Franklin, and feeding the horse was a lesson in pain with his ankle.

Brian called over his shoulder, "Hey Aaron. Come here for a sec."

****

I glanced at Old Charlie who hung his head over the paddock fence. Lilli grabbed my hand. She squeezed it and shook her head.

"We need to go so Mr. G can return before it gets dark."

"Right."

I wanted to be home with every fiber of my being, but what would Mrs. Z say about Brian? Would she understand what we'd tried to do? She'd never forgive me for leaving Brian, especially if—

How was Brian doing? I sighed. Forget Mrs. Z. I'd never forgive myself if anything happened.

Lilli had sent Aaron back to his brother at the cabin. Had he made it yet? He didn't have a rifle, so he couldn't shoot anyone else. Then there was Lilli. What would Mrs. Z say when she saw all the tattoos? She wasn't judgmental like that, was she? Bless all the goddesses, she couldn't afford to be because Lilli was saving lives. We needed her and the doctor.

Lilli walked to the truck and opened the door. I followed, my shoulders back and head tall. Was Lilli's confidence rubbing off on me? I had already learned so much, and I'd gotten a taste of helping people, really helping them, not just holding their hand while they slipped away. I needed more of that. It gave me a purpose, the power to change the fate of someone, to keep them from dying.

She turned to face me. My throat closed as I struggled under her intense scrutiny. Would I ever get used to it? I better if we were going to work together.

"What is it, Olivia? Are you okay?"

I swayed as the blood seemed to drain from my head. *Just say it.*

"I-I want to—"

Why couldn't I say it? *Because I'm afraid she'll say no.*

Lilli stared at me, her gray eyes boring into mine. She reached for my arm, and I welcomed the steady hand. Would she understand?

"Could—I—maybe—"

"Spit it out, girl." She placed her hands on her hips.

I swallowed and blurted, "Work with you in the clinic?"

Lilli cocked her head at me. "You're already hired." She squinted at me. "I thought you knew that."

"Wha—"

All the tension left my shoulders, and I climbed into the truck cab. "For real?"

She gave me a gentle shove, and Mr. G rolled down his window. "Ready?"

Lilli lifted her black bag into the bed of the truck and climbed in beside me. "You're a natural at this stuff. I'm sure Dr. N will be happy to have another apprentice."

"Oh." I put a hand to my lips. I was a natural? Why didn't I feel like a natural? "Thanks."

I sank back in the vinyl-covered seat, a smile pulling at the corners of my mouth.

"I think Olivia will make an amazing addition to your team," Mr. G said and turned the key in the ignition. "To Cedarville. You two have lives to save."

Mr. G eased his truck into gear and drove down the driveway. Old Charlie whinnied from the barn, and the farm disappeared behind the trees as we drove onto the 96.

****

The sun shone through the dirty truck windshield. Mr. Grady broke the silence. "So how did you get work with Dr. Nordby?"

Lilli wiped her nose on a tissue. "Well, that's a story, but I didn't approach her. She approached me." She chuckled.

"Do tell." Mr. G gripped the truck as it hobbled over branches and debris in the road.

"Me and Jade arrived in Franklin just after the first storms, but my mom and dad...well they found us a place above the bakery on Main Street so we'd have"—she made quotation marks with her fingers—"privacy."

"That's where you lived? With seven kids?" I gawked at her. What did I really know about this tattooed woman?

"Don't interrupt." Mr. G scowled at me.

I threw my hands up. "Fine." Storytelling had become our new television, radio, and movies all rolled into one. It was a slow and detailed form of entertainment that could fill hours, and I could tell Lilli would be a favorite storyteller at Cedarville bonfires and potlucks. I sank back into the seat as Lilli took a windup breath.

"Where was I?"

Mr. G stared at the road as he maneuvered around

potholes and large branches. "Your parents—"

"Didn't want us in their house." Lilli ran her hand over her hair and sighed. "You know, I left Jade just this morning, but bless all the goddesses, I miss that woman already."

Mr. G did a double take. "Wait. Did you say 'Jade'? Does that mean you're Emma's Lilli?"

"You know Emma?" Lilli shook her head. "Of course you do, in a town this small—"

"Yeah. Small world." Mr. G shifted the old truck to a lower gear with a metal-on-metal grind as the truck bumped around a pile of logs.

****

Josh tromped through the slushy snow and across the yard to the cabin. He stopped at the porch steps. Children's laughter came from inside. Was this the right cabin? There was smoke coming out of the chimney. He raised his hand to knock, and the door creaked open. Brian filled the doorway, favoring an ankle but smiling.

"Brian." Josh took his hand and pulled him in for a pat on the back. "Am I glad to see you. Olivia said—"

Brian jerked away and stared at Josh. "You saw her? Is she okay?"

"She's fine. Headed to Cedarville with Lilli and the meds." Josh held Brian by the shoulders, taking in all the scratches and bruises.

Dad came around the cabin and gave a low whistle. "Boy, I'd like to see the other guy." He took off his hat and climbed the steps.

Brian stood aside and waved them in. "The other guy is Mother Nature, so—" Brian shrugged and winced. "Come on in. Perry's on the couch with—"

Josh stopped just inside the door. A young man

stood behind the couch, his hair stringy and clothes filthy, and a woman knelt beside Perry Brewster.

"Is that Aaron?"

"Yes." Brian spoke under his breath.

Josh clenched his fists. The tension in the room was stifling. Would Dad tell them about their father? He sure didn't want that job.

A child pointed at him. "Who's that, Mommy?"

Josh smiled at the child. A woman sat at the table with six kids, two on each chair, and an infant in her lap. "Hi, I'm—"

Dad bumped past him to the woman kneeling beside Perry. "I'm Dr. Woolf. You must be the doctor from Franklin."

"Yes. I'm Dr. Nordby." She reached out a hand. "You must be the rescue team."

"That's us." Dad shook hands with the doctor. "We've been waiting a long time to meet you."

Perry lay sprawled on the couch, and Aaron slouched behind him.

Josh nudged Brian. "Is that—" He motioned to the woman in the kitchen.

"Jade." Brian sank into a chair.

"Bless-all-the-goddesses Lilli's Jade?" Emma was going to freak when they got home with all these kids and Jade.

Dr. Nordby gestured toward the woman surrounded by children at the table. "And these are her and Lilli's foster kids."

Josh counted three chairs, two kids per chair, and Jade held an infant. "Seven children?"

Josh took a seat next to Brian. "So, bring me up to speed." Josh shook his head.

Brian sighed. "I fell off a cliff, Perry got shot, Olivia left—"

Josh put up a hand. "No." Josh gestured to the room full of people. "Fast-forward to this."

"I'll try. The doctor, Jade, and all the kids arrived about twenty-five minutes ago, and Aaron showed up about ten minutes later. Next thing I knew, we were serving soup to the kids, boiling water on the fire, and the doctor was checking Perry's wound, then you guys arrived."

"That's Aaron, really?" Josh glared at the young man. "I didn't recognize him. He looks deflated."

Brian grimaced and nodded.

"You've been busy for someone off the beaten track. How's the ankle?"

Brian shrugged. "It'll heal. I just want to get home." He glanced at his wrist.

"Isn't that Olivia's?" Josh reached to touch the watch.

Brian cradled it to his chest. "Yes. She left it with me, and it's already 2:47."

Josh pulled his hand back. Brian must be worried about her. She'd been worried about him when they met on the road. What did that mean? "Are you and—"

Brian glared at him, and he backed away holding up his hands in surrender. He glanced at Dad who winked and stood. Would Brian ride down the mountain or demand to walk? If the steely look in his eye was any indicator, they'd better leave soon.

Josh rubbed the stubble on his chin. What would he do if Emma had left without him? He'd be pounding down the walls and making crutches.

Dr. N finished taping the bandage on Perry's leg.

"My assistant did an excellent job."

"We met her on the road. We've heard of her." Dad turned to Josh. "Tell the guys to prep for departure."

Josh opened the door and called to Stevie and Tucker waiting in the yard. "Tucker, bring the stretcher."

Dad called out the door, "Do we have two?"

"No, but I brought the sling." Stevie pulled a long black strap out of the truck.

"That will work." Josh joined Stevie and Tucker outside. "We just need to get Brian to the truck. Virg should be at the bend about a mile down the hill."

"I'll have that stretcher ready in a minute." Tucker pulled metal poles and a canvas sheet out of a tote bag. "Good thing there's four of us."

"Five with Aaron, and we have the doctor, Jade, and seven kids." Dad shook his head.

Brian stood. "What about Top Hat? We can't leave him here." He hobbled to the back door.

"Aaron can lead him down the mountain." Perry's statement hung in the air.

Brian stared at Aaron, who stared at the floor. "Do you know how to handle a horse?"

Aaron bobbed his head but didn't raise his gaze to meet Brian's.

"He'd been helping on Cooper's farm with his yearlings before Mom passed." Perry stared until Aaron's shoulders relaxed.

He was just a kid without a mom, and Josh shuffled his feet. How many times had he wanted to wring Aaron's neck? But he didn't even have a mom, and his dad was—

"I can lead a horse downhill." Aaron held eye contact with his brother.

"It's decided, then." Dr. Woolf chuckled. "We'll make quite the procession on the way home." He held out a hand to Dr. N and pulled her to her feet. "We leave in ten." He disappeared out the front door.

"You heard the man." Josh scanned the room, and his gaze stopped at the table. Jade winked at him, a small smile on her lips, but the kids stared with mouths hanging open.

Boy, is Emma in for a surprise. Josh headed out the door. It would take them longer to get home with all these people, but they were headed in the right direction, downhill.

Chapter Twenty-Nine

Brian grimaced with each lurch of the truck. It had been a long ride so far, and the bumps and twists around logs and corners in the road didn't seem familiar. He was going home, though, and O would be there. His stomach tightened. Would she be happy to see him? Would she change her mind about him? It was a long walk, after all, which would give her time to think about...

Them?

They rounded a large bend, and the valley spread out wide and green. *Home.* A warm breeze blew over him. At last, warmth.

Jade and all the kids jostled in the back seat of the double cab. They crawled over each other like a pack of pups, sometimes staring out the window at him and sometimes waving at Perry. They were making up a game and arguing over the rules, but they would giggle more than cry. Jade's voice remained calm, yet stern at times.

Brian gazed deep into the woods they passed through. These kids would never know video games, TV, radio, or refrigeration. They would amuse themselves with stories they told each other and games they invented. He missed his online gaming, but he didn't want to miss a minute of the actual trek out of the mountains.

A hawk soared overhead and squawked as it swooped up and flew over the forest. He would have missed that if he'd had his nose in a game.

His ankle throbbed, but not like it had when he was trying to climb up the cliff. Perry winced and muttered under his breath. Was he talking in his sleep? Brian turned away. They both had pain.

Brian rubbed his leg. At least he hadn't been shot. He'd always wanted a brother or sister, but after Aaron, and seeing all of Jade's kids clambering for attention? He took in the flowering trees spotting the valley. Cedarville was all the family he needed, besides Olivia.

The truck rolled along, leaving the walkers to follow. Aaron led Top Hat, and Brian could make out the white body and black head of the horse bobbing as they traveled side by side. Aaron had a hand on his shoulder, and the horse nudged Aaron's chest. Top Hat's ears were perked forward. Did he trust Aaron? It seemed so.

Aaron placed his hand on the horse's neck, his movements slow and graceful around Top Hat's face. How many times had Olivia told him, "Horses are not dogs. No sudden movements." The horse nibbled the front pocket of his flannel shirt, and Aaron laughed. He pushed Top Hat's face away. They both seemed happy.

Who wouldn't be happy? They were headed home. Brian sighed and leaned against the wall of the truck bed. Virg hit another hole in the road, and the truck lurched to the side.

"Ahh." He winced.

Josh put a hand on his shoulder. "How're you doing, Brian?" Josh sat on a wheel well in the truck bed.

Brian gave him a thumbs-up. "I'm fine, but Perry hasn't opened his eyes since we left the cabin."

"Sleep is the best thing for him."

The truck squeaked to a stop, and Josh jumped out and walked back up the road with his dad and Dr. Nordby. They waited for Tucker and Stevie to reach them. Oscar sniffed the ground around the men. Brian had wanted him in the bed of the truck with him, but he wouldn't settle down and jumped out so he could trot beside the truck.

Brian closed his eyes but still couldn't make out what they were talking about. He'd dozed off by the time Josh returned.

Brian rubbed the back of his stiff neck. Perry lay on the pillows and blankets, his face pale.

"This is Silver Springs Road. Mr. G's farm is up that way." Josh leaned back on his elbows.

"It is? I guess Olivia and I rode on the trails to Samson's farm, so—"

"Stevie's going with Aaron and Top Hat to explain things." Josh put a hand on Perry's shoulder, and Perry cracked open an eye. "Aaron's taking Top Hat home, but he wants to say something to you first."

Brian hung his head. He'd wanted to take the horse back. He'd wanted to ride down the mountain with Olivia. He'd wanted to be the one to deliver the medicine to Cedarville, but here he was helpless, unable to walk. He crossed his arms and gazed into the distance to give Aaron and Perry some privacy.

Aaron whispered in Perry's ear, and Perry nodded, his gaze on Aaron. Aaron hugged his brother, turned, and walked back to Top Hat. Perry collapsed back onto the blankets. What would Mr. G say when he saw Aaron leading his horse down his driveway? If only he could witness that little scene.

Josh settled in his spot, and Virg started the truck engine.

Josh leaned over and whispered, "We found Perry and Aaron's dad—"

"His dad?"

"His body. That's what took us so long to get to you, well, that and the storm."

"Wait. His dad's—" Brian froze. Another death. When would it end?

Perry's eyelids fluttered. Dr. Nordby had given him an injection for the pain, but he must still feel pain. The roads were rough from washouts, branches, and debris. They bumped their way down the mountain, jostling Perry's leg, but the pain of Josh's news would be far worse.

Brian glanced at Aaron who turned off on Silver Springs Road with Top Hat. He adjusted his seat, his ankle throbbing. "I don't envy the person who has to give him the news about his dad."

****

The truck brakes squealed, and Brian jerked awake. They were at the giant log pile. It had only been three days since he'd been here, but it seemed like a lifetime. He had changed. He'd kissed the girl he'd always wanted to kiss, and she'd kissed him back. Had he imagined that? Olivia was at the bottom of this hill, but who was she waiting for? His stomach clenched, and he glared at Perry.

Virg climbed out of the truck cab. Josh jumped from the truck bed and helped Jade out. She cradled the sleeping baby in her arms.

"Sorry, ma'am." Virg took his hat off and nodded to Jade. "Maybe we'll have this pile cleared in a month or two. Until then, you gotta hike to town."

"We walk from here." Dr. Woolf's voice rang out through the trees.

Brian adjusted his leg. He flinched. This was going to be a long walk.

Jade stood to the side and motioned to a toddler. "We walk from here, Willy. Come on, baby. Let the others out."

Willy glared at Jade. "I am not a baby, and I want a ride." He held his hands up to her and started to cry.

Josh put a hand on Willy's head. "You can be number one. Can you help me count?" Josh helped another child down. "Two."

"Two," Willy repeated. He had a job and swelled with importance. The kids piled out of the truck, and Willy turned to Jade. "And Thomas makes seven, right, Jade?"

Jade ruffled his hair. "That's right, Willy."

Brian would offer to carry Willy if he could, but considering he couldn't even walk without help, that wasn't going to happen. He turned to Perry and gave him a nudge. "Dude, wake up. This is where we walk."

"Huh?" Perry pushed hair from his face and wiped his eyes.

Josh opened the tailgate, and Stevie and Josh lifted the poles on either side of Perry and began to slide him out of the truck bed.

"Ahh," Perry groaned.

Brian winced. Perry wasn't such a bad guy, and he certainly wasn't a dork. Perry was a product of his circumstance, just like Aaron. Perry had tried to be Aaron's dad, but he was still a kid himself. He'd been decent, friendly even, and his sense of humor might be a bit dry, but at least he had one. *Is that what Olivia found attractive about him?*

Brian sighed and scooted to the truck gate and sat, then eased himself to the ground, landing on his good ankle. Dr. Nordby rushed to his side and adjusted the straps of the sling holding up his leg. Josh and Dr. Woolf appeared at either side.

She moved to check the straps holding Perry to the stretcher. "That should do it." She nodded to Stevie and Josh. "Don't drop him. It could reopen his wound, and he can't afford to lose any more blood. Got it?"

"I'm not making any promises," Stevie growled.

Brian opened his mouth to say something but clenched his jaw instead. What had Perry done to Stevie? Did he really want to know?

Dr. Woolf adjusted Brian's arm over his shoulder. "Okay, people. Let's move." Brian gritted his teeth. Olivia was at the bottom of this hill. With a grunt, he began the final descent to home.

Chapter Thirty

Emma coasted her bicycle down Main Street, the sun warming her shoulders. The ring on her finger glittered in the sun. She had a sheen of sweat on her upper lip as she braked at the back door of the clinic. The scent of spring flowers filled the air and brought a smile to her lips. She parked the bike and unlocked the clinic door. Voices made her pause. Dr. Johnson wasn't scheduled to be here today. Was it the new doctor?

She dashed down the hall to the front desk and stopped. "Olivia."

Olivia gave her a grin as Emma hugged her, then held her at arm's length. "Are you okay? You look so pale." She grabbed Olivia's wrist to check her pulse, but Olivia pulled away and pointed to the waiting area.

"Ahem. Emma?"

She spun around. "Lilli?"

Lilli crossed the space between them in two steps and threw her arms around her. They stood rocking back and forth.

She chuckled and finally pulled away. "This woman saved my life during the first storm." She glanced from Lilli to Olivia. "Oh, the stories I could tell about this woman."

"Now, now. I have a few stories about you too." Lilli shook her pointer finger. "Besides, that was two lifetimes ago. I'm all grown up now." She smiled. "But what's that shiny thing on your finger?"

Emma blushed. "Josh proposed."

"I met this Josh guy on the way down, but when do I get a formal introduction?" Lilli frowned with hands on her hips.

"Formal introduction? What are you, the queen of Franklin?" Olivia reached for Emma's hand.

She smiled as Lilli and Olivia shuffled to get a better view of the ring. "Ladies, please." She craned her neck to scan the clinic waiting room. "Is Jade here?" She braced herself for Lilli's answer.

"Jade is on her way, but it takes longer with the little ones." Lilli rocked on her heels.

"Little ones?" Emma's mouth dropped. "You mean children? How many?"

"Seven at last count. That's how I met Dr. Nordby." Lilli shrugged out of her parka.

She gasped. "Seven? Wait. Is the doctor here?"

"Mmm." Olivia put a hand to her head and sank into a chair.

Emma knelt beside Olivia, pressing her hand against Olivia's forehead. "You need to rest while I get Lilli up to speed." She smiled and pushed curls behind Olivia's ear. "I can't believe you're back, and you brought the meds. And Lilli? You deserve a rest."

"I'll be fine, but I can't believe you're getting married. I'm so happy for you." Olivia surrendered her naked wrist and let her take her pulse. "I'm so glad to be back. It seems like we've been out there for weeks, not days."

"It does at that." She bobbed her head as she assisted Olivia down the hall. "My office has a couch. You can lay down while Lilli and I stock the meds."

"Don't you mean gab." Olivia gave her an impish beam that caught her off guard.

She leaned her head to touch Olivia's. She'd missed this girl, and the relief at her return left her a bit giddy. What had Samson been thinking to send her up in the mountains?

"Where is Brian?" She pressed her lips together as Olivia's cheeks turned pink.

"He's coming with Josh and the rescue team."

She nodded, holding her smile from her lips. Whatever had happened between them, Olivia had survived, and that was all that mattered right now. But something happened between them.

"I've got a note from Dr. N on how to administer the meds and a chart to figure out doses by weight. We can post it in the dispensary." Lilli followed them with her bag held at her side. "But I need to hear more about this Josh fellow."

Emma smiled at how normal this all seemed, like pre-storm girl talk. They were all waiting for their someone special, Jade, Josh, and Brian. "Let's get Olivia settled. It's the least we can do for the girl who made it to Franklin, and it will keep us busy until Jade gets here."

Lilli paused in the hallway. "Jade. Yes. They should be here soon. They'll have to carry that Brewster kid and—"

"Perry Brewster? He's coming in?" Emma frowned.

Lilli's smile faded. "Gunshot wound."

Emma scowled at Olivia. "You could have given me a heads-up." She wrapped her arm around Olivia's slight shoulders. "Is Perry's wound serious?"

"Perry will live." Lilli adjusted the bag on her

shoulder.

"How do you know him?" If Perry had hurt Jade or Lilli, he'd have to answer to her.

"He stole my dad's car last November, and Dad blamed me. He always blames me. But that's over." Lilli stared at the floor tiles. "Dr. Nordby needed help with an orphaned child, and of course, Jade was all over that, and Dr. Nordby asked me if I'd come to the clinic to help her. She's been training me to be her assistant."

"That's how I got this position. Dr. Johnson needed help, and here I am." Emma shrugged. "I bet you're good at it." She helped Olivia through the narrow door. "So, does that mean you're staying?"

Lilli shrugged. "If you'll have us."

"Have you? I'm thrilled." She chuckled. This day was getting better by the minute. "We have so much to catch up on, but let's get Olivia settled first. There are sheets and a blanket in that hall closet."

She helped Olivia to the couch.

Olivia slumped into the cushions. "And a pillow?"

She chuckled and held her hand against Olivia's forehead. She was warm, but that was normal, right? The important thing was that she was back. After what she'd been through, a slight fever made sense. She placed a hand on Olivia's arm. "I'm just glad you're back and in one piece. Wait until Mrs. Z finds out."

Emma gazed at Lilli, but Lilli was staring out the front door and down Main Street. She needed Jade more than she needed air. She sighed and scanned the street for Josh. He'd be here soon, and Jade better be with him, preferably before it got dark.

****

I lay still as a stone as Emma tucked a blanket

around my shoulders, and Lilli tucked around my legs and feet. I was cocooned, and I closed my eyes with a sigh. How did I always end up on a couch in a clinic? I would have cried, but I didn't want to ruin their happy reunion.

Emma cleared her throat. "Let's get to work. I see you have your bag. Let's see the vials."

Lilli patted the black bag and bobbed her head.

"Our dispensary is this way." Emma led Lilli out of the office and down the hall.

Was I really home? Home. What a word. Four little letters packed with good food, warm fires, laughter, and all the good things. The front door opened, and someone with short steps was rushing down the hall.

"Olivia?"

Mrs. Z burst into the room, and I sat up in time for her to gather me in her arms. I didn't have the energy to chuckle. She held me at arm's length to examine me, and I laughed. She hugged me again, and I relaxed into her soft embrace. I was home.

"How did you know—" I shook my head.

"News travels fast around here." She sank onto the chair by my bed and pushed the hair out of my eyes.

"Mrs. Z. I'm so—" My throat closed.

She pulled me into another hug, and I melted into her warmth. "No talking. Only resting." She kissed my forehead. "Then we'll take you home."

"I like the sound of that." I rolled my shoulders, releasing the last of the tension I was holding. Mrs. Z winked at me.

"You sleep now." She sat in a chair by the bed and held my hand. A smooth warmth filled my chest as I closed my eyes.

****

I opened my eyes to dust motes floating through sunbeams. They shone through the window as I rose to sit on the couch. Where was I? The clinic? I rubbed my eyes. I had made it, but would Mrs. Z ever forgive me for missing the party?

The ticktock of the clock in the reception area seemed to echo in the silence. I put a hand to my lips. Brian's kiss was my second thought. It still made my tummy tingle. Two voices mingled, and Lilli's distinctive bark made me grin. Emma giggled. They must be unpacking the vials of medicines and supplies and reminiscing, maybe catching up on the past year. Had it been a year since Emma arrived? Almost a year and a half.

I swung my legs around and scooted off the couch. I wanted to help, so maybe a little snooping was in order. I opened a drawer. Pencils, pens, pads of paper, paper clips, a stapler, tape, all the office supplies a person could need. The problem was they would run out, just like the medicine. What would happen when this batch ran out?

What was that commotion? Emma's words hit me like cool water. "People are coming down the street, headed to the clinic."

I jumped up and ran to the door. Dr. Nordby was shaking hands and waving, just like a parade.

I opened the door and stood on the step of the clinic. Jade held Little Ike and led several other kids who all held hands, tagging along behind her.

I turned. "It's them, the rescue party." I scanned the street. Where was he?

Perry lay on a stretcher carried by Stevie and Josh, and Dr. N walked beside them.

Dr. Woolf helped someone who hobbled along beside him.

"Brian." I took a step, but Lilli pushed me aside and ran to Jade. I opened my mouth to scold her, but the vision of her pulling Little Ike into her arms took my breath away. She kissed Jade, then bent down to hug the other kids, and I couldn't do it. My eyes met Brian's, and he took another unsteady step.

Emma pushed past me to Josh, and I opened my mouth to object, but I stared mesmerized as Josh set down the stretcher and wrapped his arms around her. Was that what I wanted from Brian? I stood frozen on the step. Why did my stomach flutter? I stood as people emerged from houses and yards to greet the rescue team and meet the new doctor. The laughter and shouts grew in volume, and I glanced at Brian who had been swallowed by the crowd.

I took a step, then another, pressing through my neighbors and friends, until I was standing in front of him. His gaze burned into me. Had I really called him a Dorkmeister? If I could take back one word—

Brian reached for my hand, and a jolt ran up my arm. He pulled me closer, and I closed my eyes as he kissed me lightly on the lips. I leaned into him and opened my eyes. His face was swollen and bruised, and I ran my fingers over the lump on his forehead. He winced but didn't pull away. His lips were soft as he kissed me again. We weren't the only people on the street, but Brian was the only person I wanted to see, to hold, to—

"Whoa. PDA?" Perry gave Brian a lopsided grin.

I blinked and gazed from Brian to Perry. Perry had lost his mystique, for sure, but he wasn't such a bad guy. Dr. Woolf walked over to Perry. "Carry this one to my house."

"Right, boss," Tucker said.

"We need to talk." Dr. Woolf followed Perry's stretcher carried by the rescue team. They disappeared around the corner.

I stared after Perry and Dr. Woolf. "What was that all about?"

Josh shook his head. "A lot has happened in the last three days, and I don't envy Dad right now."

"Why?" Emma asked.

"We found Frank Brewster's body on our way up the mountain."

I gasped. "Their dad died? Is that why—"

"The last thing he needs is the whole town listening in while Dad tells him." Josh pecked Emma on the cheek. "I'll see you soon." He turned and followed his dad.

Dr. N joined Lilli and Emma. "This is the woman I was telling you about." Lilli pointed to Emma. "She's been assisting Dr. Johnson and is basically running the clinic by herself."

"Well, it's time you had a little help." Dr. N shook Emma's hand.

"I'm so happy to meet you." Emma clasped her hand. "And to see Lilli and Jade again, and all their kids." She led the doctor inside. Lilli and Jade filed into the clinic behind them, with the kids following like ducklings.

I glanced at Brian, and goose bumps ran up and down my arms. We were alone. Would he kiss me again? *Maybe I'll kiss him.*

I put my hands on either side of his face. "You made it. You're home."

He pulled Grandpa Billy's watch from his wrist and

glanced at the time. "5:26. I hope I'm not too late."

"Never." Warmth enveloped me, and I grinned like a fool.

"I told you I would never leave you." He pulled me into his warm, strong embrace and kissed me until my thoughts whirled, and my head spun.

Mmm. I could feast on this banquet of consequences.

Chapter Thirty-One

The bell on the clinic door jangled, and a woman my mother's age limped into the Cedarville Health Clinic.

"Morning, Olivia." She smiled and took a seat.

I scanned the list and put a check by Dr. Delores Woolf. "Morning, Dr. Woolf."

"Delores, please."

Dr. N and Lilli had been in town for four days, and the waiting room was filled with people. I pulled her chart and carried it to the holder on a door. I gave it a quick glance before slipping it into the holder: knee sprain. That explained the limp.

The scarf Delores wore matched her red blouse with a pattern of sleek, black cats. Her stylish flair stood out amongst the blue jeans and gray, navy blue, or black jackets.

"Don't sit down yet, Delores. Lilli will see you now. Let me help you." I put my arm out, and she wrapped hers through mine. I helped her down the hall and into exam room three.

"Thank you, Olivia. You're good at this, you know?"

I smiled at her, a warm glow filling my chest.

"How is Mrs. Zadinsky? Has she forgiven you for venturing into the mountains yet?" Was she biting her lip to hide her smile? I helped her onto the exam table.

I chuckled but hesitated before I answered. "Mrs. Z still informs me every time I walk into a room that I 'could have died out there.'" I made the quote sign for Mrs. Z's words. She was mad, and that made sense to me, but why did she have to complain to the whole town?

"Give her time. She cares about you, that's all."

She did care, but I hated the frown she directed at me every day. I shrugged. "I keep reminding her that I did return with the medicine, Lilli, and the doctor. Still, she just rants about me gallivanting up and down the mountains in a snowstorm without a care in the world."

Delores's laughter rang off the walls of the small examining room. "Sounds just like her."

I admired her steady gaze and her strong hands, so like Mom's. The reminder hurt me all the same. I adjusted my faded purple scrubs. "Lilli will be in soon."

She massaged her left knee and smiled at me as I closed the door silently and walked back to the front desk. Lilli appeared at my side. I jumped and spun.

She took the chart from me. "Is Delores in room three?"

"Geez, Lilli. Yes, she is, and are you trying to give me a heart attack?"

She wiggled her eyebrows at me and disappeared into exam room three. I sighed and walked to the front desk. With Lilli around, who needed excitement?

The bell on the door jangled. Emma burst in and shed her jacket. I rubbed the brown stain on the hem of my scrubs. It came with the job, but how were Emma's scrubs so crisp and spotless?

"Hey, Olivia. Jade is bringing Ike for a quick check. He has a fever. Do we have an opening later this morning?"

I nodded. "I'll put him on the schedule with Dr. N. I know how Lilli is with her own kids."

Jade managed all seven kids with a grace and patience that was a mystery to me. She single-handedly ran her little band of orphans as if she'd done it all her life, while Lilli worked at the clinic from dawn to dusk. Jade's soft Southern drawl floated through the neighborhood as she strolled with the children in the evening. She'd name the trees and the plants as they walked, giving a hug or a kiss when someone tumbled.

I added Ike to the schedule, then copied Dr. N's notes to another patient's file. Everything was handwritten these days. I shook out my aching fingers.

Dr. N poked her head out of the office. "Olivia, next patient, please. Emma, prep room five."

Emma rushed down the hall. The clinic door opened with a tinkle.

"Well don't you look official." Mrs. Z's voice held the authority of a woman yet to forgive me.

I tensed and glanced over my shoulder at her. Wait. What? Was she holding a cake? And why was Mr. G, Samson, and Barb—

Gracie ran to me, and I hoisted her up for a hug.

"Happy birthday." She grabbed my face in her tiny four-year-old hands and kissed my cheek.

"Thank you, Gracie." I hugged her again. She squirmed to be put down and ran back to Barb. "How did you know?"

Mrs. Z placed the cake on the counter, a twinkle in her eye. "You missed your party, even after you promised you wouldn't." She shook a finger at me. "That is unacceptable, young lady." Her lips twitched with the beginning of a smile. Maybe she could forgive. She pulled out a box of wooden matches and lit the one and only candle. Birthday candles, another casualty in the supply chain debacle that was our post-storm normal.

I blinked, trying to hold back the tears. "For me?"

"The Happy Birthday" song filled the room as sunbeams shone through the dusty windows. Brian walked through the door on his crutches, and my throat constricted.

Brian kissed my cheek, and I squeezed his hand. "I heard rumors of a surprise party at the clinic."

My face hurt from smiling so hard, but I couldn't stop. He hadn't forgotten my birthday, but I thought Mrs. Z had. I stared at the cake she'd promised me, the scent of real sugar filling the clinic. My mouth watered.

"Thank you everyone."

What a year. This was the first birthday where I really did feel different, but in a good way, more mature, more confident. An exam room door opened, and I glanced down the hall.

Dr. Nordby stuck her head out of room five. "Olivia, could you bring me the tray I prepared?"

Ah, yes. I was still at work.

"Coming." I turned to the small group of friends. "Thank you so much, everybody, but I—"

"You're working, and the doctor needs your help. We know." Mrs. Z gave a brisk nod to Mr. G and the Coffeys. Brian squeezed my hand, then took Mrs. Z's arm. She made her way out the door, my party filing out with her. Brian balanced on his crutches as he helped her down the two steps to the sidewalk. Oscar sat on the sidewalk, his pink tongue hanging out as he panted. He never let Brian out of his sight.

"Olivia?" Dr. N stood in the hallway waiting.

"Coming, Doctor." I glanced over my shoulder but couldn't pull my gaze from Brian as he ran his long fingers through the tangle of hair on Oscar's head.

Those same fingers had held my face as he kissed me. Lightness filled my chest and radiated to my fingers and toes. I would never have made it to Franklin without him. He was the real hero. I balanced the chrome tray with Dr. N's equipment on one arm and headed down the hall.

End Notes

The 7 stages of grief
1. Shock and denial
2. Pain and guilt
3. Anger and bargaining
4. Depression, reflection, and loneliness
5. Upward turn
6. Reconstructions and working through
7. Acceptance.

A word about the author…

Avis M. Adams writes poetry and fiction and has two YA novels released by The Wild Rose Press, *The Incident,* and *The Disappearing Names.* and she has a romance novella, *The Christmas Wish Knotts* as well. *Quilcene*, a collection of her poems was released in 2019. She teaches English at a local community college and belongs to two fabulous critique groups. She is an active member of Willamette Writers and lives in Portland, Oregon, where she writes, hikes, kayaks, gardens, and spends time with her granddaughter.
https://avis-m-adams.com

Thank you for purchasing
this publication of The Wild Rose Press, Inc.

For questions or more information
contact us at
info@thewildrosepress.com.

The Wild Rose Press, Inc.
www.thewildrosepress.com